CHARRED BY DARKNESS

BOOK THREE
DRAGONS OF ETERNITY

ALEXANDRA IVY

Charred by Darkness
© 2017 by by Debbie Raleigh

Editor: Julia Ganis
– JuliaEdits.com

Cover Art by Patricia Schmitt (Pickyme)

Formatting by
Sweet 'N Spicy Designs
– http://sweetnspicydesigns.com

http://alexandraivy.com

CHAPTER ONE

Levet appeared at the entrance of the dragon's lair with a dramatic flutter of his wings. He was a gargoyle who liked to make his entrance in style. And really, who could blame him?

Okay, there were a few stupid demons who had called him a sorry excuse for a gargoyle. And he'd even been voted out of the Gargoyle Guild, just because he barely stood three feet tall and his magic wasn't the traditional, boring gargoyle magic.

But whatever he lacked in stature, or magic, he more than made up in sheer magnificence.

His features were gloriously grotesque, and he had the traditional thick gray skin of all gargoyles. His eyes were reptilian and his horns were stunted. He even possessed a long tail he kept polished until it glowed.

Even more superb, his wings were brightly colored

and delicate as gossamer. The haters might claim that they would have been more fitting on a sprite or fairy than a lethal creature of the dark. But as far as Levet was concerned they only added to his air of sensuous mystery.

Waiting for the door to be swept open, Levet gave a sniff of disapproval.

Really, it was too bad of Tayla. He'd been having a perfectly lovely time with a fire imp when his friend had sent him a frantic mental plea for him to join her at Synge's lair.

Pinto.

No, wait. That wasn't right.

Pronto. He snapped his fingers. *Oui*, that was it.

The least she could do was be standing there, awaiting his arrival with bated breath.

This had to be the work of Tayla's new mate, Baine, he decided, wrinkling his snout. When he'd first met the pretty imp, Tayla had been hiding from the lethal dragon. They'd lived together in a pretty tea shop where Tayla had cooked him delicious treats.

He sighed. He missed those days.

Now Tayla was all googly-eyed over her mate, with no time to provide Levet with hot scones and his favorite nectar. It was a tragedy.

Perhaps he should return to the volcano where his fire imp was waiting for him. The way she could singe his—

Levet's naughty thoughts were interrupted when the thick stone wall slid inward. He hesitated before he waddled forward. There was no point in putting off the inevitable. The quicker he could discover what Tayla needed, the quicker he could return to his lovely imp.

There was the fresh scent of citrus, then a female appeared out of the darkness.

Tayla.

She was lovely. No surprise—all fey tended to be blessed with exquisite beauty.

Today she was wearing a loose white tunic that flowed to the floor in a shimmer of silk. Her dark gold hair was fanned over her shoulders and down her back with hints of fire in the strands. Her face was a pale oval with a narrow nose and plush peach lips. Her eyes were a pale green with shards of jade, and thickly lashed.

At the sight of him she held out her hands. "Oh, Levet. Thank the goddess."

Levet reached to grasp her fingers. "I do not think you need to thank the goddess," he assured her. "It was my kind and generous heart that brought me here."

He believed in pointing out his accomplishments. How else could other creatures properly appreciate his many talents?

Tayla's lips twitched as she released his claws and waved him into the cavernous space.

"Yes, well. I should warn you that things are a tad…" She paused, before she cleared her throat and continued. "Tense today."

Levet stepped forward, his wings snapping together as the wall slid closed behind him.

Heat and smoke and a hint of brimstone curled around them. It was smothering.

"This is a dragon's lair. When are things not tense?" Levet pointed out.

"True." Tayla wrinkled her pretty nose. "Let's just say that things are more tense than usual."

Levet scowled. "What the devil is wrong with the dragons? Not only did Baine steal you away from me, but his father just had his mate and daughter returned to him. The old lizard should be delighted," Levet groused, still annoyed with having his comfy home disrupted when Baine had come to claim Tayla in return for her father's debts.

Tayla paled. "Shh. If Synge hears you..." She allowed her words to trail away. Almost as if she decided that she was wasting her breath. She gave a shake of her head before turning to lead Levet deeper into the lair. "Never mind. Follow me."

Levet hurried to keep up with his hostess, his claws scraping against the stone floor. Unlike Baine's palatial home, his father, Synge, preferred a more rustic style. Barren stone. Heavy wooden beams on the ceiling. Torches dotting along the walls. Screams from the torture chambers.

Very medieval.

Of course, the older dragon had a few spaces that were actually decorated. His throne room. And the harems. And, Levet assumed, the family chambers.

Mostly, however, it was all very dark and grim.

Just like Synge.

They moved quickly down a long corridor where a few servants were going about their business. Some were half-breed dragons, and others were fey or vampires. All of them were wearing green and gold uniforms with the emblem of a lightning bolt on their upper chest. And all of them looked nervous. As if they were expecting to be torched by dragon-fire at any moment.

Waiting until they turned into a hallway that Levet suspected led to the private quarters, he moved to walk at Tayla's side.

"So what has Synge's tail in a twist?" he asked.

Tayla cast a furtive glance around before answering. "Blayze disappeared."

Levet scratched his stunted horn. How long had it been since they found the female dragon. A day? Two days?

"Already?" he asked in surprise. "Do not mistake me—I assumed she would fly the coop, just not so quickly."

Tayla's breath hissed between her teeth as she glared down at him. "Are you deliberately trying to get yourself killed?"

Levet considered. Why were people always asking him such a ridiculous question?

"Non." He gave a decisive shake of his head. "Not deliberately."

Tayla briefly closed her eyes, her citrus scent filling the air. Then, with seeming effort, she opened her eyes and continued down the hallway.

"We don't think that Blayze willingly left the lair," she said.

Levet blinked. Then blinked again. Although he'd been busy with his imp when Blayze had been returned to this lair, he'd heard that they'd tucked her away and surrounded her with layers upon layers of magic. Not to mention the fact that no one could get in or out of a dragon's lair.

"She was kidnapped?"

Tayla bit her bottom lip. "It's impossible to say."

Levet gave his horn another scratch. "I fear that I am confused, *ma belle*," he said. "Perhaps it would be best if you started at the beginning."

She slowly nodded, her green eyes shimmering with worry in the torchlight as they turned down a new corridor. This one had a faded fresco on one wall. It looked like it depicted a battle between dragons and a legion of trolls.

The dragons were winning.

Predictable.

"You know that Blayze was cursed just hours after she was born?" Tayla was asking him.

"Oui. A most cowardly act." Levet's tail twitched. He hated demons who picked on the most vulnerable. "What despicable monster would torture a mere child?"

Tayla's hands clenched into tight fights. "Demons are rarely known for their warm and fuzzy personalities."

"Hey, I can be warm," Levet protested. He glanced down at his leathery, gray skin. "Not so much fuzzy."

"Levet," Tayla chastised, her tone sharp. "I need you to concentrate."

Levet's wings fluttered, his lower lip jutting out in an impressive pout. Then, realizing that Tayla was genuinely worried, he heaved a small sigh.

Later he would remind her that he was a Knight In Shining Armor who was deserving of groveling respect. For now he would put aside his pride and offer his assistance.

It's what Knights In Shining Armor did.

"Pardon, *ma belle*," he said. "I am listening."

She grimaced, as if regretting her sharp tone, but she continued with her story.

"Ravel escaped with Blayze after the Dragon Council commanded that the young hatching be put to death."

Levet rolled his eyes. "Dragons."

Tayla sighed. "Yes. They are ruthless."

Levet snorted. "Ruthless does not adequately capture their essence." He glanced toward the fresco splashed over the wall. They'd reached the part of the painting where the trolls were being toasted into piles of ash by the dragons that circled overhead. "They are savage, deranged, bloodthirsty maniacs."

Her lips parted to argue. Then she gave another sigh. Not even a female besotted with her mate could pretend that the dragons were anything but brutal killers.

"Some of them," she agreed, giving a dismissive wave of her hand. "Anyway, after Ravel returned to this lair with Blayze, they called on Char to use his magic to slow time. They had to find a way to keep the stasis spell in place until they could figure out a more permanent solution."

Char, a dragon half-breed, had technically been given to Baine by his father. Like a scaly, fire-breathing birthday gift. But Levet had spent enough time in Baine's household to know that Char was considered more a brother than a servant.

The two male dragons had been BBFs for centuries.

Now Levet blinked in shock.

"Char can slow time?" he demanded in surprise.

"His mother was a Dalia demon," Tayla explained.

Ah. Levet gave a nod. Dalia were fey creatures that usually hid in the frozen tundra of Siberia. They could slow time by casting a spiderweb of power.

"Very rare," he breathed, more than a little annoyed. He'd never seen Char alter time.

Which seemed excessively unfair.

"Yes," Tayla said.

Brushing aside his irritation, Levet concentrated on more important matters.

"Did Char kidnap Blayze?" he asked.

Tayla flinched. "He's being blamed."

"But you do not believe he is guilty?"

"Char has been my mate's most loyal servant for five centuries." Her features hardened, her steps slowing as they neared the end of the corridor. "Baine is certain he couldn't be involved."

Levet tilted his head to the side. "And you?"

"I agree with Baine."

"Because you are a dutiful mate?"

She regarded him with a steady gaze. "Because I know Char. He's charming, arrogant, and self-indulgent, but there's nothing more important to him than his loyalty."

Levet sorted through his various memories of the half-breed dragon. Tayla was right. Char was arrogant.

Of course, his intelligence was doubtful, since he consistently refused to admire Levet's astonishing skills.

But the one thing he could not deny was that the younger dragon was obsessively loyal to his master. There was nothing he would not do, including giving his own life to protect Baine.

The thought that he would kidnap Baine's own sister and make an enemy of Synge was unimaginable.

They stepped through the arched opening at the end of the hallway into a small antechamber. The walls had been smoothed and polished to reflect the overhead chandelier that burned with a hundred candles. There were two long benches spaced around the floor, as if this was some sort of waiting room.

Levet's gaze darted toward the heavy wooden doors cut into the walls. He suspected that each led to a separate area of the private chambers.

The scent of ancient incense was thick in the air, along with a potent musk of a pureblood dragon who was headed in their direction.

Levet's tail twitched. It wasn't that he was afraid of the overgrown lizards. Of course he wasn't. He was a renowned hero who feared nothing.

Still, he preferred to spend his time with pretty fire imps who toasted his body with pleasure, not screaming agony.

He cleared his throat, studying his companion with a curious gaze.

"While I am quite flattered by your invitation, I fear I am not entirely certain why you were so insistent that I come."

Tayla stood in the center of the chamber, her face pale as she twisted her hands together.

"I'm worried about Char and Blayze," she told him. "We must find them."

Levet stepped forward, sensing there was more than

just concern for the two missing dragons.

"Why me?"

Tayla did more hand twisting as she carefully chose her words. Levet felt a tiny pang. He might have resented Baine for crashing into Tayla's teahouse and sweeping her away, but he never doubted that the dragon cherished Tayla with every beat of his serpentine heart. And, more importantly, he'd watched as Tayla had bloomed from a shy, skittish fey into a contented female who faced the world with confidence.

Seeing her once again nervous and on edge troubled Levet.

"Baine and his father have just started to form a relationship," she told him. "Now they're once again barely speaking. Synge is convinced that Char is guilty and he's furious that Baine refuses to agree with him." She sucked in a deep breath. "The sooner we can prove Char wasn't responsible, the better."

Levet grimaced. He could understand her sense of urgency. Dragon family dynamics were volatile under the best of circumstances. Now they must be downright explosive.

A very good reason for a smart gargoyle not to get involved.

"Surely Synge's servants are searching for them?" he suggested.

"Of course, but they're concentrating on how Char could have slipped out of the lair unnoticed." She sent him a pleading glance. "I want to discover if something else could have come in and snatched them."

"That seems unlikely."

"No more unlikely than Char betraying Baine."

Levet couldn't argue with her logic. "You want me to search the lair for an intruder?" he pressed.

She gave a lift of her hand. "I want you to search for the truth."

"Even if Char is responsible?"

She nodded without hesitation. "Yes."

Levet heaved a sigh. Only a fool meddled in dragon business, but he was no match for her big green eyes that silently begged for his help.

"Très bien." He gave a resigned lift of his hands. "I need to be taken to the place where they were last seen together."

She tossed him a relieved smile before she turned and headed across the floor.

"Through here," she said, pushing open a door.

Levet followed in her footsteps, peeking into the room.

It was a massive space that was carved out of the stone in the shape of an octagon. Overhead, the domed ceiling was covered with tiles made from gold. There was a delicate painted screen that divided the main room from a small garden at the far end where a fountain shimmered in the glow of the numerous candles.

Levet stepped forward and then came to a sudden halt. He shivered as a heavy sense of doom wrapped around him.

"I feel as if a troll is sitting on my head," he rasped.

Tayla wrapped her arms around her waist. "You can still feel Blayze's curse. It makes the atmosphere a bit heavy."

He tried to ignore the darkness that hammered at him.

"That is like saying a bear is poopy when he is in the woods."

Tayla's brows tugged together. "I don't know what that means."

Levet wrinkled his snout. "Me either. But it something that I heard at The Viper Pit," he said, referring to the vampire bar where he used to be a welcomed guest.

Okay, perhaps *welcomed* wasn't the precise word.

Grudgingly not eaten when he came through the door might be more accurate.

Levet was distracted from his inane thoughts when the darkness in the room was overshadowed by a thunderous power that made the floors tremble and the air sizzle with heat.

His claws dug into the marble floor. *A dragon.*

And one who was wielding enough magic to make Levet's skin prickle with warning.

A shadow fell across the doorway even as the air continued to heat, making Levet's wings flutter with discomfort. Really, dragons could be the most inconsiderate creatures. If he wanted to feel as if he was being roasted alive, he would return to the volcano.

On the point of complaining, Levet snapped his lips shut as a male stepped through the door and moved to stand in the center of the room.

Baine.

The dragon had chosen his familiar shape. He had a narrow face, with Asian features and almond-shaped eyes that burned with an amber fire. His straight black hair fell with liquid-smooth perfection to just above his shoulders. He was attired in nothing more than a loose pair of dojo pants that revealed the tattoos crawling over his pale skin with a strange metallic shimmer. Someone not accustomed to the markings could easily become hypnotized by their beauty as they pulsed and changed colors.

The symbols represented the knowledge that Baine had managed to acquire over his long life. Like a moving library.

On steroids.

Levet's snout twitched at the pounding smell of power and incense and magic.

Folding his arms over his chest, Baine studied his

mate before turning his attention to Levet.

"Now isn't the time for a visit," he growled.

Tayla moved forward, laying her hand on the male's arm. "I asked him to come."

The dragon flicked a brow upward, his gaze lingering on Levet's lumpy features as if searching for mold. Levet sniffed. He hadn't had mold on his face since he'd fallen asleep on top of a church in Amsterdam for a few decades.

"Why?" That was Baine. A dragon of few words.

Of course, when you could breathe fire, you didn't have to say much.

Levet sniffed. "Since when does Tayla have to ask permission for a visit from her favorite demon?"

The brow inched even higher. "Your skull is even thicker than I suspected if you believe that you're her favorite demon."

Levet scowled, but before he could retort, Tayla was speaking.

"Levet has a talent for seeing through illusions."

Baine turned his attention back to Tayla. "So does Ravel," he reminded her, referring to Blayze's mother.

Tayla shook her head. "No, she has a skill for creating them."

Baine paused, considering her words before he gave a decisive nod of his head.

"That's true," he admitted. "But I still don't understand why you would ask the gargoyle to come here."

Concern darkened her eyes as Tayla studied her mate's grim features.

"We have to do something, Baine," she said in soft tones. "For the first time in centuries you have a relationship with your father. I can't bear to see that destroyed because of a mistake."

The air sizzled with a blast of heat. "It's not a

mistake," Baine rasped. "Char would never have kidnapped Blayze."

Tayla moved back to her mate, laying her hand on the center of his chest. The tattoos whirled over his skin at a dizzying speed.

"I believe that. With all my heart," she told him. "But we have to have actual proof for Synge."

The dragon's lean features softened, his fingers lightly touching Tayla's cheek. "And you think this creature can help?"

"Hey—" Levet started to protest only to snap his lips shut when the burning amber gaze swiveled in his direction. He was fearless, not stupid. Baine was clearly on edge, causing the air to snap, crackle, and pop with his power. "I am a demon with many talents," Levet grumbled.

Tayla gave his wing a small pat before lowering her hand. "If Char didn't kidnap Blayze, someone must have entered the lair and taken them both."

Baine's brows snapped together. "Impossible. No one can enter a dragon's lair."

Tayla sent her mate a wry glance. "I did it."

"That's only because you're special."

A flush touched the imp's cheeks even as she gave a shake of her head.

"I'm happy you think I'm special, but we both know I'm not unique."

Baine stiffened. "Do you think another fey with royal blood might have snuck in?"

She gave a shrug. "Perhaps. Or it could be a demon we don't even realize has the same powers as me."

Baine was silent a long moment, a tendril of smoke curling from one nostril.

"What can the gargoyle do?" he demanded. "If there was an intruder, I would have caught their scent."

"Not if they had the ability to cover their presence

with an illusion."

Another pause. Then the dragon offered a grudging nod. "Fine. He can offer his assistance."

Levet narrowed his gaze. Pompous jackbutt.

No, wait. Jackass. *Oui.* That sounded better.

But even as he prepared to inform the ancient demon that he had better things to do than poke around a smelly dragon lair, he caught Tayla's pleading glance.

"Bien." Levet squared his shoulders. He deeply disliked dragons. Almost as much as he disliked vampires. But he would do whatever possible to ease Tayla's anxiety. "Let me do my thing."

Levet closed his eyes—he'd discovered that it offered a more dramatic effect—then he held out his hand and slowly circled the room. Behind him, Levet could hear Baine muttering beneath his breath.

He caught the words *ridiculous* and *pest.* Typical dragon. Jealous of another male who clearly possessed the superior talent.

"He really is the best at detecting illusions," Tayla loyally assured her companion.

Determined to live up to Tayla's faith in his skills, Levet fiercely concentrated on his surroundings.

Not an easy task. The lair of a dragon was filled with a variety of demons, which meant there were a hundred different types of magic that threaded through the air. Plus, Baine's thundering power was battering against him like a jackhammer.

He moved toward the bed in a far corner, his snout wrinkling. The curse swirled around the area like a nasty shroud. Poor Blayze. Her life must be a sheer horror. And now she'd been taken by—

Levet came to a halt, slowly bending down to touch the scorch marks that marred the floor next to the bed.

"Here," he said.

Tayla moved to stand next to him with a swish of

satin. "What is it?"

His brow furrowed as he allowed the lingering magic to settle inside him.

"It is not precisely a portal, but there was some sort of opening created."

Tayla crouched down beside him. "Fey?"

Levet shook his head. "Dragon."

There was a shocked silence before Tayla released a harsh sigh.

"Crap. I was so sure that Char was innocent." Tayla straightened.

Levet barely heard her low words. His attention was focused on the muted hum of power he'd very nearly missed.

"There's something else," he said in absent tones, feeling tugged across the room by the strange vibrations.

Tayla followed behind him. "What is it?"

Hmm. A most intriguing question.

It wasn't an illusion, he decided, his claws clicking on the floor as he moved toward a wall at the end of the room. Or a spell. It was more an echo of magic.

"It's ancient," he at last decided, lifting his hand to touch the floor-to-ceiling tapestry that covered the wall.

It was different from those in the hallway. This one was brighter, with scenes of children playing in a sunlit garden. He would wager his favorite Backstreet Boys poster that this work of art had been chosen by Ravel, not Synge.

Tayla brushed her fingers over his wing. "Levet?"

"Were these Blayze's original rooms?" he asked, scrunching his snout as tingles of power shot through his arm.

The tapestry wasn't responsible for the magic he was sensing.

"Yes," Tayla said. "Why?"

Grasping the ancient fabric, Levet gave a sharp tug

to bring it tumbling to the ground. Tayla made a choked sound. Perhaps she was worried about the cloud of dust that was staining her pretty tunic. Or more likely she was considering the fiery death that Synge would bestow on anyone who dared to desecrate his beloved daughter's room.

Levet was more concerned with the polished stone wall. "There is something here," he announced, his tail slashing across the floor as he took a step forward.

Baine walked to stand directly behind Levet, his heat searing across Levet's wings. Next time he visited a dragon lair he intended to bring a bag of marshmallows to toast. The annoying beasts were arrogant, selfish, and lacking in the most basic understanding of good manners.

The least they could do was provide him with a yummy snack.

"I don't see anything," Baine said.

"I'll show you." Levet sucked in a deep breath and gathered his powers.

"No," Baine snapped. "Your magic is—"

"Stupendous," Levet interrupted, tapping the tip of his claw against the wall. At the same time, he released the magic that bubbled deep inside him.

There was a giddy rush of anticipation, then, without warning, it burst out of him with more force than he expected.

Not that it was his fault. Perhaps his control over his magic was a tad sketchy. Okay, it was a lot sketchy. But he couldn't be held responsible for the fact that it actually exploded when it encountered the spell that lingered on the wall.

There was a detonation that made Levet's ears ring, and chunks of stone showered down from the ceiling. At the same time the floor cracked beneath his feet, as if the lair was about to split open and drop him into the pits of

Hades.

There was a low growl from the dragon behind him. "Shit," Baine rasped. "My father is going to kill us."

Tayla tried to soothe her furious mate. "Not if we find Blayze."

Levet ignored them both, his gaze captured by the shimmering hieroglyphs that were suddenly visible on the wall.

Ha. He knew that he'd sensed something.

Belatedly noticing Levet's remarkable discovery, Baine and Tayla moved to stand directly beside him.

"What is that?" Tayla demanded.

Levet traced one of the hieroglyphs with the tip of his claw. They looked like they'd been singed into the lower half of the wall.

"Ancient rune marks," Levet said, his voice distracted.

"A part of the curse?" Tayla pressed.

Levet shuddered, abruptly pulling his claw away from the wall. There was a pulsing darkness in the markings.

"Oui," he breathed, rubbing his claw on the side of his leg, trying to rid himself of the cloying evil that emanated from the runes.

Baine made a sound of surprise. "You discovered the curse?"

"Just an echo of it," Levet corrected.

"Explain," Baine commanded.

Levet frowned. "This is the residue from the original curse."

The tattoos beneath Baine's skin swirled as he sent Levet an impatient frown. "That isn't an explanation."

Levet scowled, glancing toward Tayla. "Does he have to be here? I can't concentrate with an overgrown lizard breathing down my neck."

She heaved a sigh, as if dealing with two males was

more than any poor imp should have to endure. "Please, Levet, this is important."

Levet flattened his lips, forcing himself to turn back toward the seething dragon.

"When the curse was cast, it imprinted itself on the wall," he explained.

"Cast?" Baine narrowed his amber eyes. "Are you saying the curse came from a witch?"

"It was designed by magic." Levet considered for a long moment. There were many creatures capable of creating a spell. Including dragons, the fey, and gargoyles. But he would have been able to detect their lingering scents. The fact that no trace remained indicated it was probably from a human. And that whoever it was had already died. "The most likely creator was a witch," he decided.

Baine studied him with a suspicious gaze. Then, seeming to decide that Levet wasn't yakking up his chin—no wait, that wasn't right...yanking his chain...*oui*, that was it—the dragon glanced toward the wall.

"Why didn't we see the runes before?"

Levet shrugged. "The curse must have been designed to conceal all traces of it."

Baine lifted his hand, holding it near the wall, but wisely not touching it. Levet grimaced. He could still feel the lingering evil.

"If we get rid of the runes, will that break the curse?" the dragon demanded.

"No." Levet waved his hands toward the runes. "The marks are just the residue from the casting. You must discover the original object that held the spell and destroy it."

Tayla's brow furrowed. "If the witch is dead, how are we supposed to discover the object?"

"Find the creature who cast the curse," Levet told

her. "They must still have the vessel used to contain the magic."

"The witch—"

"Created the spell," Levet interrupted. "It was another who cast it."

Tayla slowly turned. Levet felt his heart drop at the sight of the unreasonable hope etched on her pretty face.

He might be a hero, but he couldn't perform miracles. At least not with a dragon breathing down his neck. It was very unnerving to have a female regarding him with that particular expression.

"Can you tell who it was?"

Levet swallowed a sigh and closed his eyes. The curse had been cast centuries ago, but the sheer power of the spell had been massive. Whoever had cast it must have left behind at least a small portion of their essence.

He concentrated on the area around the wall, sorting through the various scents laced through the room like a tangled road map.

It might have been an impossible task, but Levet suspected that the rooms had been sealed shut after Ravel had left with Blayze all those years ago. There was a thick emptiness between the various layers.

Concentrating on the unmistakable chill he'd just discovered, Levet did his best to ignore the power that beat through the room like a drum.

Was Baine deliberately trying to distract him?

Foolish creature.

Bending down, Levet drew in a deep breath, isolating the scent until he was certain it was the one attached to the spell.

"A vampire," Levet at last announced, opening his eyes to glance toward Tayla.

He was expecting amazement. Awed wonderment. Perhaps even a shower of kisses.

He had, after all, just solved a centuries-old

mystery.

At the very least there should be squeals of delight.

Instead Tayla was glancing toward the door with wide eyes.

A bad feeling settled in the pit of Levet's stomach as he turned to see what the imp was staring at. Only then did he realize the cause of the excessive power that throbbed through the room.

Now there wasn't just one dragon, but two.

The new one was a large, brutish male with short black hair and eyes the color of liquid silver. He was wearing a loose pair of cargo pants and his chest was left bare to reveal his bulging muscles.

Synge.

"The vampires took my baby?" he said in low, awful tones.

Tayla took a step forward. "No, sire."

Synge pointed a finger in Levet's direction. "He just said that a vampire cursed her."

Tayla held up a hand, almost as if she was trying to calm the ancient dragon. "It's possible, but—"

Flames danced over the dragon's skin, scorching the floor and reminding Levet why he hated being around dragons. They were forever spouting fire.

So rude.

"I'll kill the bastards," Synge roared, before he was pivoting on his heel to storm away in dramatic fashion.

"Shit." Sending Levet a withering glare, Baine was hurrying from the room in the wake of his father.

Levet breathed a small sigh of relief. The air had finally cooled to a bearable level.

"Where are they going?" he asked Tayla.

She bit her lip, her face oddly pale. "I would guess that Synge intends to start a war with the vampires, and my mate is trying to halt the looming genocide."

"Ah." Levet considered for a minute, then with a

small shrug, he headed toward the door. "My work here is done," he said. "Now I intend to return to my fire imp and her toasty bed beneath the volcano."

Already busy imagining the lovely imp, Levet had reached the middle of the room when Tayla rushed to stand directly in his path.

"No," she breathed.

Halting, Levet regarded her in confusion. *"Non?"*

"We have to do something to avoid disaster," Tayla told him. "You have to convince Synge that you aren't certain the vampires are responsible."

Levet waited for the punch line. He rarely understood the jokes among other species, but he was polite enough to laugh when it was expected.

But Tayla continued to stare at him with an expectant expression. *Mon dieu.* She was serious.

"Talk to an enraged dragon?" He gave a sharp shake of his head. "And people call me locomotive."

The pretty imp heaved an exasperated sigh. "Loco," she muttered in impatient tones.

"*Oui*, loco." Levet waved an impatient hand. "I prefer to keep my bits and pieces un-singed."

Tayla pressed a hand to her stomach, the scent of lemons bursting through the air. She was genuinely afraid.

"Maybe Baine can stop him," she said, her voice uncertain.

"Let us hope so," Levet said. "The peace treaty that was signed between the dragons and vampires a thousand years ago is the only thing that has kept this world from being bathed in bloodshed."

Tayla made a sound of distress, and Levet belatedly realized he had made a strategic mistake. He should have tried to convince Tayla that all would be well. That Synge could rampage all he liked without fear of reprisal.

Instead he'd reminded her of the dire consequences of a war between the dragons and the vampires.

"You have to warn the Anasso," she abruptly decided, referring to the leader of the vampires by his formal title.

Levet's wings twitched. He hadn't confessed to his friend that he was currently avoiding Styx.

He cleared his throat. "Actually that would be a most unwise idea."

Tayla frowned. "Why?"

"The thing is that Styx might be the teeniest bit unhappy with me," Levet admitted.

Tayla rolled her eyes. "What did you do?"

Levet resisted the urge to ask why she would assume it was his fault. After all, Styx could be such a baby. Typical vampire.

"I might have put his absurdly large sword up for bid on eBay," he reluctantly confessed.

Tayla sucked in a shocked breath. "You didn't."

Levet thrust out his lower lip in an aggrieved pout. "I merely wished to see how much an enterprising demon might get for the thing," he said. The ancient weapon had just been hanging on the wall in Styx's lair. It wasn't as if he was using the thing. "It was quite astonishing. I could be a very wealthy gargoyle if Styx was not such a selfish creature."

Tayla rolled her eyes. "You must have a death wish."

"*Non*, I do not," Levet assured her. "Which is why I prefer to avoid the vampires until their tempers cool." He considered a minute. "Perhaps in a few centuries."

CHAPTER TWO

Char had always prided himself on his ability to roll with the punches.

What choice did he have? From the time he was very young, he'd understood his life as a half-breed dragon meant he would be controlled by others. First his father had bartered him to Synge to repay a debt. And then Synge had offered him to his son, Baine, as a personal guard.

But while other males might have resented their fate, Char had decided to embrace what he was given.

He might be a servant, but by the time he'd arrived in Baine's lair, he'd already developed an easy charm that made him a favorite among the other warriors. And, of course, it didn't hurt that he was capable of shape-shifting into an elegant male with sculpted features, pale silver-blond hair and gray eyes that sparkled with humor.

The female dragons were usually eager to ensure that he never felt as if he was less than equal to any other male.

His luck had continued over the years, as he'd developed a relationship with Baine that went way beyond master and servant. The two males were as close as any brothers. But still Char had remained prepared to adapt to the inevitable changes in his life.

And they'd arrived.

Baine had found his mate. A lovely imp, who would no doubt start producing babies. And unlike most dragons, Baine would be a doting father who didn't sell his offspring to the highest bidder.

Char wasn't sure what that would mean for his own place in the household, but it was certain to be different.

Still, it was all good. He was a guy who understood how to adapt and overcome.

Until this moment.

Right now he didn't know what the hell was happening.

One minute he was standing next to Blayze's bed, and the next, the world around them was fading to black.

Just for a second, he thought he must be dying. What else could explain the encroaching darkness and the sensation that the floor had disappeared and he was floating through space?

It wasn't a portal. He'd traveled through hundreds of them in his long life. He'd even visited Hades on a dare from Baine—a journey he never intended to take again.

But this was different. He felt as if he was melting along with the room, his very being dissolving into nothingness.

He couldn't tell how long he drifted in the nothingness before the world once again became solid.

It was almost as disconcerting as the melting.

One minute he was weightless, and the next his feet were hitting a marble floor with enough force to send him to his knees. He grunted in pain, his mind scrambling to clear out the fog.

It was still dark, but it was the darkness of natural shadows, not...well, whatever had surrounded him before.

Holding up his hand, he allowed flames to dance over his skin as he cautiously rose to his feet.

He was in a large octagonal chamber. It looked similar in size and shape to the room he'd just been zapped out of, only it wasn't lavishly decorated. At least not yet.

Glancing around he could see the domed ceiling was in the process of being covered with priceless golden tiles, while the heavy furniture and tapestries were carefully stowed in the corners of the space.

What was going on? Was this some sort of illusion meant to deceive his eyes?

On the point of moving toward the door on the far wall, he came to a sharp halt as he caught sight of an object lying on the stone floor.

No. Not an object.

Blayze.

Shit. It hadn't occurred to him that she might have been sucked up in the same magic that was affecting him. Stupid, of course. Why would anyone go to the effort of wasting their power on him? He was just a servant.

But Blayze...

She was priceless.

Not only was she a rare, pureblood female dragon, but she was the daughter of Synge. One of the most powerful dragons in all the worlds.

With a blur of motion he was moving to kneel at

her side, studying her delicately carved features.

The slender nose, the full lips that were the color of summer roses. The pale, creamy skin that sharply contrasted with the ebony darkness of her hair that spilled across the stone floor in a river of silk.

Just like the first time he'd seen her lying unconscious in her bed, the sight of her punched him in the gut with stunning force.

It wasn't her beauty. Dragons better than any other creature understood the outer shell was meaningless. They could alter their shape on a whim.

No, it was her inner essence that reached out to touch the dragon within him.

Char grimaced, squashing his renegade blast of awareness.

This female was destined to become the mate of a powerful, pureblood dragon. The only reason he'd even been allowed close to her was because Synge had been desperate to slow time until they could find a way to break the curse that had been placed on her when she was just a hatchling…

Char hissed in shock. The web of magic he'd spread over Blayze had been disrupted when the darkness had filled the room. So why couldn't he sense her curse?

"Blayze?" Holding up his hand that still glowed with flames, he leaned forward, barely resisting the urge to brush his mouth over the soft temptation of her lips. "Blayze, can you hear me?"

Nothing happened for a tense minute, then the long, luxuriously thick lashes slowly swept upward.

Char felt another punch to the gut. Her eyes were magnificent.

They were so pale they looked white, and were flecked with shimmering dots of color. Like the finest opals.

His dragon roared in pleasure, the heat of his beast

thundering through the air. *Dear goddess.* He'd never come so close to losing control. And he wasn't even touching her.

Thankfully unaware of his blistering reaction, Blayze studied him with a strange calm.

"Who are you?"

"Char," he said. "I was asked by your father to protect you."

Her gaze wandered over his face, her nose flaring as she breathed in his scent.

"A half-breed," she murmured.

Char jerked back, his bemusement shattered by an icy chill. Quite an accomplishment for a dragon who had flames dancing through his veins.

"I prefer to be called Char, not half-breed," he said in clipped tones.

She continued to study him, either indifferent to his irritation or just oblivious to it. "What is your magic?"

"My mother is a Dalia demon."

"Dalia." She tested the name on her tongue before she gave a slow nod. "You stopped time."

"Technically, I just slowed it," he corrected.

"It was enough."

With a grace that marked her as a pureblood dragon, Blayze was suddenly rising from the floor. The beaded gown that she'd been wearing when she was brought back to her father's lair rustled like a musical instrument in the silence, the scent of exotic spices teasing at his senses.

Char straightened, stepping away from her slender body.

"Enough for what?" he demanded.

Blayze moved to inspect the room, although her delicate features were impossible to read in the darkness. "For me to step outside my curse long enough to concentrate."

Char stiffened. "You created the illusion."

She moved to stare at the heavy wooden chairs that were pushed against the wall.

"There is no illusion," she said.

Char's irritation changed to annoyance. Okay, his dragon might be desperately in lust with the female. And there might be a strange tug of connection that was even more troubling.

But he wasn't her servant. And he wasn't going to be treated as if he was.

"Then what did you do to the room?"

She glanced over her shoulder, her pale eyes swirling with pinpricks of color.

"Not what. When."

Char scowled. "What are you talking about?"

She continued her circuit of the room, absently stroking her fingers over a marble statue that looked as if it'd been plundered from an ancient Greek garden. It probably had.

He remembered it sitting beside a lattice wall at the other end of the space.

"I took us back in time."

Char hissed in shock. Was she serious?

"Did you just say you took us back in time?" he demanded in disbelief.

She moved toward the carved headboard that was a part of her bed, her brow furrowed as if she was troubled by the sight of it.

"Yes."

"How?"

She stared at the wall, seemingly lost in her thoughts. "I grabbed onto the threads of the curse and pulled us backward," she answered in absent tones.

"You pulled us backward in time by using the thread of a curse." Char tried to wrap his brain around the mere thought.

He'd never heard of anyone capable of moving through time. Perhaps a Jinn. Or an Elemental creature.

But not a dragon.

"Isn't that what I just said?" She didn't even bother to glance in his direction.

Char flatted his lips. Damn Torque. If his friend hadn't suggested that Char could help keep Blayze in stasis, Synge would never have demanded that he travel to his lair and stay with his daughter.

He could be enjoying time with his fellow guards. Sparring in the gym. Or eating a massive meal and drinking too much nectar. Instead of standing in this dusty room, trying to squash the urge to ram his head into the nearest wall.

"Just how far back in time did you take us?"

She wrinkled her slender nose. "I intended to bring us to the night that my father formally celebrated my birth."

Char grunted in shock. He wasn't entirely sure how old she was, and he wasn't stupid enough to ask. But if she wasn't completely out of her mind, then he was currently in a time before he was even born.

The thought made his poor brain spin.

"Listen—" He started to say, only to be interrupted when Blayze tilted back her head, her nose flaring as if she caught a sudden scent.

"He's here," she murmured, rapidly heading across the floor.

"Wait." Char moved to stand directly in her path. "Where are you going?"

She frowned, as if baffled by his perfectly reasonable question.

"To find me."

"To find you?" Char knew he sounded like a parrot, but dammit, he'd just been tugged through time on the thread of a curse. Who could blame him for being a little

29

rattled?

"This is the nursery," Blayze told him, speaking slowly as if he was especially stupid. "I need to find out why I'm not here."

She stepped forward, clearly expecting him to step out of her way. Typical dragon arrogance.

Char, however, stood his ground, his expression set in stubborn lines.

"Later," he insisted. "First we need to discuss this."

"There's nothing to discuss."

His jaw tightened. "Humor me."

She sent him a glance filled with baffled frustration. "We're wasting time."

Char refused to back down. "If we need more, you can always give another tug on the thread, right?"

She stilled, easily sensing the edge in his words. "Does it bother you?"

He released a humorless laugh. "To be whisked through a half dozen centuries? Yeah, a little."

"But you are capable of manipulating time."

Char shook his head. It took every ounce of his power to slow time for a day or two. He couldn't imagine the magic necessary to transfer two dragons through several hundred years.

"Not like that," he muttered, giving a wave of his hand that was covered in flames. "But that's not what I want to discuss."

Her eyes reflected his dragon-fire, emphasizing the dazzling kaleidoscope of colors.

"Well?"

Char released a slow breath, trying to restrain his inner beast who was desperate to reach out and stroke the pearly luster of her skin. Was it as soft as it looked?

"Can we sit?" he abruptly demanded.

"Char—"

"Please."

With the sort of sigh that women learned in the womb, she pivoted on her heel to take a seat on one of the heavy chairs against the wall.

"Fine." She folded her hands in her lap and eyed him with impatience. "Tell me what you want to know."

Char frowned as he settled on a seat next to her. He was suddenly struck by an odd realization.

Since they'd been jerked back through time he'd been too distracted to actually consider the fact that Blayze had spent most of her existence in hiding, completely isolated to prevent anyone from realizing that she was still alive.

He would expect her to be confused, even terrified, at being taken out of her mother's protective magic.

Instead she was completely coherent and focused on her goal with an alarming intensity.

"Tell me everything," he commanded.

"Excuse me?"

He waved a hand. "Start at the beginning."

She sent him a puzzled glance. "What beginning?"

"When you were cursed."

"Oh." She shrugged. "I was too young to really understand what was happening. All I truly recall is that I was lying in my bed when I was hit with an unbearable pain."

"The curse?" he asked.

"Yes. Things got very fuzzy, and the next thing I knew I was in a secluded lair and I was wrapped in my mother's magic."

Char studied her in amazement. Her tone was calm, almost matter-of-fact. If his life had been destroyed by an evil curse he'd be screaming in fury.

"You were kept asleep?"

She glanced away, her dark hair sliding over her shoulders in a river of ebony.

"It's difficult to explain. The part of my mind that

was compromised by the curse was kept in stasis, but my mother was able to keep our mental connection open," she said.

"She could communicate with you?"

"Not only that, she allowed me to see the world through her eyes."

Ah. Well that would explain why she seemed so comfortable to be out of her stasis. Still, it must have been horrible. To be able to see the world and yet know you were trapped by an evil curse.

Char felt a strange tug on his heart. Was it sympathy?

He studied her elegant profile. "I thought she remained in hibernation with you?"

"For the most part she did, but she was anxious to discover who cursed me," she told him. "At least once a year she would leave me hidden in a secret lair, and try and find some clue."

"What did she find out?"

"Nothing more than she already knew." She turned back to reveal her shimmering eyes. "I was cursed on the night that my father celebrated my birth."

Char gave a slow nod. That made sense. Female dragons were rare. Synge no doubt had been eager to display his glorious prize.

Blayze was worth a fortune.

The lair would have been overflowing with guests. What better opportunity to slip into the nursery and unleash the curse?

"She didn't learn anything?"

Her shoulders slumped, and Char sensed that a part of her…dimmed.

Caught off guard, he released the flames that danced around his fingers, allowing the shadows to return. Sure enough, a faint glow surrounded Blayze's slender body. Like a soft halo of white light.

His inner beast stilled, intrigued by the sight. Dragons could create fire. They could breathe it with destructive force. They could allow it to move over their skin. And mold it to use as a weapon.

But they didn't glow.

This was caused by her magic. Or perhaps, her very essence.

"No one was willing to discuss that night or who might want to punish my father," she said in sad tones.

Char could no longer resist temptation. Reaching out, he allowed his fingers to smooth through the warm silk of her hair, tucking the heavy strands behind her ear. Even through the darkness he could easily make out her pale features.

He hissed in pleasure, then with an effort, he forced himself to concentrate on her words.

"No one could help?"

She slowly reached up to brush his fingers that lingered on her cheek. Not knocking them away, but almost as if she was trying to process the feel of his touch.

Char abruptly wondered if he was the first male beyond her father to ever lay a hand on her.

"Everyone claimed they hadn't seen or heard anything," she said.

He frowned. Even if the lair had been stuffed from top to bottom with demons, Synge would never have left his daughter unguarded.

Not for a second.

"What about your father's servants?" he demanded.

"They swore that no one was seen going in or out of the nursery."

"So either they're lying or the demon responsible for cursing you was capable of entering the nursery without being seen."

She nodded, her expression revealing that she'd

already come to the same conclusion.

"After centuries of waiting for my mother to find the truth, I decided to take matters into my own hands."

"Even though you were kept in hibernation?"

"I had nothing else to do but study the curse," she reminded him. "Eventually I realized that I could use my powers to follow the magic back through time. So I decided that's what I would do."

Char felt a cold chill inch down his spine. He discovered he didn't like the thought that she might have come to this place—or rather this time—without him.

"Then why did you wait?" he asked.

"My mother's power kept me in a protective bubble that was intended to shelter me, but it also kept me trapped." Her hand dropped away from his fingers. "And when I escaped her powers, the curse's madness made it impossible to focus my thoughts long enough to explain what I wanted to do."

Her eyes sparkled with pinpricks of light and Char could feel the frustration heating her skin. A frustration she'd no doubt endured for centuries.

"And then I arrived," he said.

A smile curved her lips and Char caught sight of a dimple that danced in her cheek. Yet another enchanting surprise.

"Yes. I finally had the opportunity to use my magic."

His fingers brushed down her jaw, savoring the feel of her skin. The glow that surrounded her abruptly brightened, and Char felt a tingle of pleasure.

The pretty dragon liked his touch.

"What exactly is your magic?" he asked.

She hesitated, as if wondering whether or not to tell him. "I don't actually have any powers," she finally admitted. "At least not in the traditional sense."

Char arched a brow. "Now I'm intrigued."

"I can't create magic, but I can see it, and sometimes I can manipulate it."

"Manipulate it?" He gave a confused shake of his head. "What's that mean?"

"It's difficult to explain. When I concentrate, I can see magic like strands of music." She lifted her hands, waving them in a graceful motion. Like a conductor directing an unseen orchestra. "They're like strands that float through the air in various patterns."

Char studied her in fascination. "And you can manipulate them."

"Not if it's just a quick spell. Something that is there and then gone." Her brow furrowed, as if she was struggling to think of the words to explain her talent. "But if it's a magic that lingers or if it's a permanent part of an object, then I can use my powers to touch and alter the threads."

Char gave a nod. It would be easy to assume that her powers were disappointing for a purebred dragon. There were dragons who could change iron to gold. Or create earthquakes that could smash entire cities. Or even control the minds of massive hordes of demons to force them to do their bidding.

Hell, Char was a half-breed and he could slow time.

But anyone who assumed her powers were somehow inadequate would be wrong.

The ability to manipulate the magic of others meant that her powers were limitless. As vast and infinite as magic itself.

"Like you traced the threads of your curse," he said. She nodded. "Yes."

He studied her in confusion. "But you can't break it?"

"No." The opal eyes flared with brilliant colors. "I've tried for centuries."

He turned his head to glance around the empty

room. "Why did you bring us to this time?"

"I didn't mean to bring you."

Char felt that same blast of annoyance at the thought that she might have disappeared without him.

He told himself he was simply worried about her safety. Who knew what was just beyond the door? Probably the crazy-ass demon who'd cursed her in the first place. Or maybe something worse.

She was a fool to rush into an unknown situation without backup.

But he knew that wasn't what was bothering him.

He resented the thought that she regarded him as an unwanted companion. Like he was some bug that got stuck to her shoe and now she was trying to scrape him off.

"We're in this together now," he informed her, his tone indicating that he wasn't arguing the point.

She blinked, studying him with that strange, calm intensity. "I suppose so."

A rueful smile twisted his lips. He didn't think she was deliberately trying to bash his pride. It was more a lucky accident.

"So, what was your plan?" he asked.

"I realized that if I could move backward in time, I didn't have to worry about how to break the curse," she told him. "I could simply stop the spell before it ever happens."

CHAPTER THREE

The Viper Pit in downtown Chicago was renowned among demons.

The ritzy club was hidden behind a subtle glamour that made it look like an abandoned warehouse. It was the best way to keep away humans and other riffraff. Once past the illusion, however, the public rooms spread out like a palace.

There were acres of marble floors dotted with white fluted pillars, and glittering chandeliers that hung from the impossibly high ceiling. A dozen fountains sprayed droplets of water between the white-clothed tables that were surrounded by the crowd of demons.

In the back of the club was a wide doorway that gave access to the basement. The lower rooms were reserved for the gaming tables, as well as for those searching for more intimate entertainment. There were private rooms where they could join in the ongoing orgies or start one of their own.

The upper balcony was reserved for the vampire owner of the club, Viper, and his exclusive guests. Tonight, his guest was Styx, the Anasso, the King of Vampires.

Hidden by the crystals of a large chandelier, Levet studied the two powerful vampires.

Viper possessed the haunting beauty of all vampires. His hair was long and as pale as moonlight. A direct contrast to his eyes that were as dark as midnight.

Tonight he was attired in a cherry-red velvet coat that flowed nearly to his knees, and black satin breeches that looked more suitable for a Regency ball than a Chicago nightclub.

Styx had chosen his usual black leather. The six foot five vampire had long black hair that was braided and decorated with turquoise beads. He had the narrow, bronzed features of his Aztec ancestors. And the temper of a rabid hyena.

They were currently sharing a bottle of brandy from Viper's private stock. Levet's mouth watered. He'd occasionally managed to sneak a bottle or two from the cellars, but it had been months since he last—

A ripple of darkness shot upward, bringing a sharp end to Levet's distraction.

Sacre bleu.

He'd had little choice but to sneak into The Viper Pit. The vampires were a prickly bunch, and they had an annoying tendency to hold a grudge. Really, you would think they had never heard of the golden rule to "forgive and forget." If he wanted to warn Styx about the dragons, then he would have to find a way to force him to listen.

Then, as occasionally happened, Levet had found himself distracted.

A lethal mistake, as Viper moved with blinding

speed, leaping upward to grasp Levet and yank him out of the chandelier.

"Well, well. Look what I discovered, amigo," Viper drawled, holding Levet by the horn like he was a sack of potatoes. "It appears that I have bats in my belfry."

Styx slowly rose to his feet, the lights suddenly flickering. The Anasso's anger could take out entire grids of electricity.

"It's kind of chunky to be a bat," Styx retorted.

Viper smiled, displaying his snowy white fangs. "And his wings are entirely too frilly. Just like a dew fairy."

Levet struggled, even knowing it was a futile effort. It was the principle of the thing.

"They are not frilly," Levet muttered, his tail twitching.

Viper lifted Levet higher, twirling him around.

"What do you think, oh mighty master?" Viper mocked. "Do you proclaim them frilly?"

Levet caught sight of Styx rolling his eyes. The ancient vampire hated to be reminded that he was king. It was a position that was more a duty than a pleasure. Still, the annoying creature was happy enough to poke fun of Levet.

"Yeah, they're frilly," Styx agreed.

"There," Viper said. "It's been proclaimed."

Levet scowled, hoping the crowd of demons that were carousing below could not see his humiliation. He did have a reputation to protect.

Giving another wiggle, Levet glared at his tormentors. "Release me or I will tell Shay you are being mean to me again."

Viper hissed, his lips pulling back as his fangs lengthened. "Do you want to kill him, or can I do it?" he asked his overly-large companion.

Levet flapped his wings. *Oops.* Perhaps it was not

the best strategy to threaten to tattle to Viper's pretty mate, Shay. The male was a little sensitive about the fact that Levet was a favorite with the females. "Wait," he demanded.

Styx ignored him, folding his arms over his massive chest. "He did try to sell my sword."

Viper shrugged. "Yes, but he wrecked my favorite car."

"True. Still, I—"

"The dragons are coming to start a war," Levet hastily interrupted.

He did not think that the two vampires would actually kill him. But it might be best not to take the risk.

A sudden chill saturated the air as Styx stiffened. "Is he drunk?"

"I don't think so." Viper held Levet closer, pretending to study him. Then he sniffed his breath. "Hard to tell with a gargoyle."

Levet gave an annoyed wave of his hands. "I am serious. You must listen to me."

"Must?" The chill was beginning to frost Levet's tail as Styx narrowed his eyes. "Do you think you can give me orders?"

"Fine." Levet made a sound of resignation. What did he care if the dragons and vampires decided to have a war? It was not as if it mattered to him. "Then be turned into piles of ash. See if I care."

There was a tense silence before Styx muttered a curse.

"Release him," he abruptly commanded.

Viper scowled. "Are you serious?"

Styx gave a nod. "Yes. If this is another of his idiotic tricks, then you can rip off his head."

"You swear?"

"On my honor."

Levet felt himself being unceremoniously dropped

to the ground. With a flap of his wings he managed to land on his feet, sending his two tormentors a glare.

"Vampires." Sheer disgust edged his words. "You are as bad as dragons."

Styx towered over him, his lean face hard with warning. "Start talking."

Levet sniffed, heroically resisting the urge to blow a raspberry toward the arrogant beast. He had to try and think of Tayla. His friend was depending on him.

"Perhaps you have heard of Synge?" he instead asked.

"Baine's sire," Styx retorted.

The dragons rarely interacted with this world, but Levet wasn't surprised the vampire was familiar with the various names and clan connections. It wasn't just Styx's big sword that made him the natural leader of the vampires.

"*Oui*," Levet said. "The ancient dragon was recently reunited with his daughter, Blayze."

"I'd heard rumors that she was found by Tayla along with a tribe of Sylvermyst," Viper murmured. The silver-haired vampire traded in information along with pleasure at his various clubs.

Styx nodded. "Isn't she the one who was cursed?"

"Unfortunately," Levet said.

Styx regarded Levet with a smoldering impatience. "What does that have to do with the vampires?"

"A few hours ago, Blayze disappeared from her father's lair," Levet explained.

Styx arched his dark brows. "Dragons don't just disappear. Not unless they want to."

"So far it is a mystery." Levet puffed out his chest. "Which is why they sent for *moi*."

"You?" Viper's disbelief was palpable. "The dragons asked you to come to their lair?"

Levet pursed his lips. He didn't know why it was

surprising. He was, after all, a renowned Knight In Shining Armor.

Why wouldn't the dragons send for him when they needed a hero?

Then he recalled that it wasn't precisely the dragons who'd wanted him to travel to their lair.

"Actually…" He cleared his throat. "It was Tayla who offered the invitation."

Styx took a minute to connect the name with a demon. "The imp who is mated to Baine," he at last said.

"And my friend," Levet added with pride.

Styx didn't appear nearly as impressed as he should be. Instead, he continued to study Levet with seething impatience. "Why would she send for you?"

Levet puffed out his chest even farther, nearly popping a rib out of place. "She desired me to use my awesome skills to discover who'd kidnapped Blayze."

Viper snorted, but it was Styx who asked the obvious question.

"And did you discover who was responsible?"

Levet hesitated. He was getting to the part where he needed to choose his words with care. See—he did not have a death wish.

"Well, I was in the process of searching for an intruder when my magic shattered an illusion that was hiding the origin of Blayze's curse."

Styx and Viper exchanged a glance. The sort of glance that implied they were dealing with a creature who was not entirely sane.

"Do you know what the hell he just said?" Viper drawled.

Levet shook his head. "Barbarians."

Styx abruptly sliced his large hand through the air. "Get to the point."

"I exposed the magic responsible for the curse," Levet continued. "It was obviously a spell created by a human, but I could detect that a vampire had been the one to cast it."

Styx looked confused. "How could you know that?"

Levet gave a wave of his hand. "When the spell exploded it left tiny bits of the vampire's essence embedded in the wall."

The Anasso grimaced, but he didn't press for details. Vampires possessed a deep, abiding hatred for magic. It was the one thing that their considerable powers couldn't control. They couldn't even detect it.

"What does this have to do with Blayze's disappearance?" Styx demanded.

"I am not certain. I was attempting to explain what I had discovered, but like vampires, a dragon cannot allow a demon to finish a sentence," Levet complained, hunching his shoulders. "It was not my fault."

Viper tilted his head to the side. "What wasn't your fault?"

"Synge happened to walk in while I was offering my big revolt."

"Reveal," Viper corrected with a roll of his eyes.

"*Oui*. Big reveal." Levet waved a dismissive hand. "All the stupid creature managed to hear was that a vampire had cursed his daughter."

Realization of the massive danger about to descend on them hit the two vampires with visible force. Viper cursed. But it was Styx's surge of icy power that made the club suddenly fall silent.

No one within a six-block radius could miss the Anasso's displeasure as the lights sparked and then went dark.

"Shit," Styx growled.

Levet took a strategic step backward. It wasn't that he was scared of the vampires. Of course he wasn't. But he was small, and Styx had feet the size of tanks. He might get squashed as the male paced from one end of the balcony to the other.

"It is not my fault," Levet reminded the furious vampires.

"Where is Synge?" Styx demanded.

Levet lowered his gaze, pretending to study the floorboards beneath his claws.

"Levet, answer the question," Viper snapped.

Levet heaved a sigh, reluctantly lifting his head to meet Styx's frigid gaze.

"I am not certain, but Baine was following him," he confessed. "Perhaps he has managed to calm the—"

His words were interrupted as the entire building was suddenly shaking like it'd just been hit by an earthquake. Only Levet knew it wasn't a natural force that was making the floor tremble beneath his feet, and the chandeliers sway from side to side. Not when the air was sizzling with a heat that could only come from a pissed-off dragon.

Styx sent him a narrow-eyed glare. "You were saying?"

CHAPTER FOUR

Blayze was trying not to be overwhelmed.

It was unexpectedly difficult.

After all, it was one thing to experience the world through the eyes of her mother. There was a constant buffer between herself and actually being awake and fully aware of the sensations that battered against her. But now she was left raw and exposed.

And it didn't help to have Char standing just a few inches away from her.

She'd seen other dragons through her mother's eyes, but never one who was this gorgeous. His gray eyes that darkened from silver to smoke, the blond hair that was short enough to emphasize his finely carved features. And his hard, male body.

He was deliciously sexy.

Was it any wonder her dragon was anxiously pressing against her skin, wanting a taste?

With an effort, she battled the urge to reach up her hand and touch the warm skin of his face.

She'd risked everything to travel back through time. She couldn't allow herself to be distracted from her goal.

Later she would indulge in her new, unexpectedly sensual attraction toward Char.

"You hope to discover who cursed you before it can happen?" the male was asking, his brow wrinkled.

"Yes." She didn't understand why he looked so confused. It seemed the obvious solution to her. "I know the exact time I was cursed. And I thought I knew the exact place."

His lips flattened. "A dangerous plan."

She shrugged. I didn't matter if it was dangerous. Not if it could work. "It was the most logical way to get rid of the curse. But now..." Her words trailed away as she glanced around the room in disappointment.

"But what?" her companion prompted.

She grimaced, her mind racing. Had she changed the past simply by coming back in time? It was a possibility.

"I should be here," she said, pointing toward the spot where her bed was located in the future.

Char took a long minute. He had a sour look on his face. The same look her mother had when she wanted to scold Blayze. The male, however, was smart enough not to waste his breath.

"Perhaps you're sharing your mother's room," he instead suggested. "It looks as if this nursery is still being refurbished."

She wrinkled her nose, walking toward the distant wall. She'd spent centuries being hidden by her mother. Usually in some remote pocket between dimensions. But she'd instantly sensed when she'd been returned to her childhood room two days ago.

It'd been in the scent of incense in the air. The

warmth of her father's power.

And the evil that continued to pulse in the air.

"No. I could *feel* the curse," she insisted, placing her hand against the wall. "Here. This is the place it was cast. Which means that I should be here."

Char glanced toward the empty wall before offering a small shrug. "Clearly something is wrong. We need to go back."

She continued to run her hand over the smooth stone. "I can't."

The male made a sound of annoyance. "You can't? Or you won't?"

"Can't."

There was a dramatic pause. "Are you telling me that we're stuck in this time?" the half-dragon finally asked.

She nodded. "Yes."

Heat swirled through the air, the certain sign that Char was struggling to contain his temper.

"Perfect," he snapped.

She studied him, still unaccustomed to being battered by such intense emotions. She'd been protected for so long it was fascinating.

And slightly irritating.

"I told you I didn't mean for you to come with me."

His eyes shimmered with a brilliant silver fire as he stepped toward her. "Stop saying that."

Her lips parted to—

Well, she was going to say something, but she forgot exactly what it was as he swooped his head downward and covered her mouth with his own.

Blayze froze. Not in panic. Or fear. Or even outrage.

Nope, it was pure, undiluted pleasure.

His lips were hard, demanding a response even as his hands stroking through her hair were unbearably gentle. Deep inside, her dragon purred, seduced by the taste of his kiss. Fire. Spice. And the bubbling effervescence of his fey magic.

Intoxicating.

Briefly forgetting her determination to concentrate on her reason for traveling to this particular time and place, Blayze lifted her hands to lay them against his chest. She could feel his heat searing through the thin white shirt, but it wasn't enough. She wanted to stroke her fingers over his bare flesh. And to arch her body against his hard muscles.

But her lack of experience made her feel awkward and uncertain.

Should she wiggle her hands beneath the shirt? Or did she just rip it off?

She was still floundering for an answer when Char ended her dilemma by slowly lifting his head to stare down at her with a brooding expression.

Disappointment cascaded through her. Tilting back her head, she fought to leash her inner beast.

"Why did you stop?" she demanded.

"Because I shouldn't have started in the first place," he growled, his voice rough. "But you're like my grandfather's demon brew."

Blayze blinked. She knew that demon brew was a potent liqueur made by orcs, but she didn't know what that had to do with her.

"Is that good or bad?"

"It's…intoxicating. Like drinking wildfire." He gave a small shake of his head. "But it always ends up with a nasty hangover," he rasped, his eyes smoldering as he brushed his fingers over her cheek. Her lips parted, but once again he halted her from speaking by lowering his head and pressing a short, searing kiss on her mouth. His hands framed her face, his heat blasting around her. "Hell," he muttered against her lips. "What am I doing?"

"Kissing me," Blayze told him, wondering if he was as confused as she was.

Her brain was spinning in a strange but wonderful way, making it hard to think clearly.

"You're a pureblood," he breathed.

"And you're a half-breed."

"Exactly."

Her brows pulled together in confusion. "I don't understand."

"Your father would turn me into a crispy critter if he ever discovered I had dared to touch you," he explained.

Blayze took an abrupt step backward, shaking off his lingering touch. Over the centuries she'd been cocooned from the world, but the one thing she'd always been perfectly clear about was the fact that Synge had agreed with the Dragon Council to have her destroyed when she was just a babe.

"Don't call him that," she commanded.

Char studied her with a puzzled frown. "What?"

"He's not my father."

"Blayze?"

Char's voice was laced with concern, as if he was worried she wasn't entirely stable.

"Synge was willing to stand aside and allow me to be destroyed," she said, the room glowing as white flames danced over her skin. "I have no loyalty to my sire."

Reminded of why she was there, Blayze pivoted on her heel and headed toward the door. She was out of the room and marching up the narrow corridor before Char managed to catch up with her.

"Hold on, Blayze," he said in low tones, reaching to grasp her arm. "There's something going on."

Coming to a halt, Blayze belatedly caught the distant sounds and scents that she could sense were coming from Synge's throne room.

"A party," she murmured.

Char's fingers tightened on her arm. "We can't just waltz around without a plan."

"Shh." She motioned Char toward an open door. "Someone's coming."

In silence they entered the small room that appeared to be some sort of storage area.

Char pushed the door until it was left open less than an inch. It made it impossible to see who was strolling down the hallway, but Blayze could easily determine that it was two female dragons.

She could also hear their conversation despite the fact that they were speaking in whispers.

"I wish I had known that it was going to be such a grand event," the first female complained.

The second female clicked her tongue. "Well, it is Synge. He must always be outlandish. Whether it is conquering another clan or announcing that his mate is pregnant with a female."

Blayze stifled her gasp. She suddenly realized why her private chambers hadn't looked familiar.

She hadn't been born yet.

"It is more than that." Female One intruded into Blayze's shock.

"What do you mean?" Female Two asked.

"Did you not notice the number of Council members who have arrived?"

"Well, a pureblood daughter is a rare event," Female Two pointed out.

There was the sound of a *swish swish swish* as the females' silk skirts brushed against the tiled floor of the corridor. They were nearly level with the room where Blayze and Char were hidden.

"I heard a rumor," Female One coyly teased her companion.

"Really?" Female Two's voice was breathless. It reminded Blayze of her mother's warning that a dragon's lair was a maze of dangerous politics. Power bases were not only created by sheer strength, but by the treaties between clans. And, of course, the ability to appear utterly invincible. "Tell me."

"My mate believes that Synge might be attempting to challenge one of the Council members for their position."

Blayze frowned. She'd never heard her mother mention that Synge had ambitions to become a Council member.

"He does possess an obscene hoard," Female Two murmured.

"And a vast number of warriors," Female One added.

There was more swishing as the dragons passed the storage room, headed toward the throne room.

"But if he intends to challenge for a seat on the Council, then why would he invite the members to his lair?" Female Two finally asked an intelligent question.

"Intimidation," the first female said. "And..." She allowed her words to trail away.

"What?" her companion prompted.

"My mate has heard that Synge intends to announce the betrothal of his daughter tonight," Female One revealed in dramatic tones.

Blayze sensed Char stiffening, but she kept her attention on the voices that were starting to fade as the females continued down the corridor.

"A betrothal before she is even born?" the second one asked.

"Yes."

Char made a sound, but Blayze strained to hear what the first female had to say.

"If he has managed to capture the heir to a powerful

clan that would all but ensure that Synge could simply demand a seat. Who would be foolish enough to stand against him?"

"I should have chosen a better gift," Female Two muttered, then their voices vanished into the flood of chatter spilling out of the throne room.

Blayze was trying to sift through what she'd heard when she felt her arms being grasped in a firm grip so Char could turn her to meet his furious glare.

You have a mate?"

CHAPTER FIVE

Char knew he was being ridiculous.

There were a thousand things wrong with this scenario.

He was standing in Synge's lair centuries before he was ever born. Surrounded by dragons who would happily destroy them if they decided they were intruders. And they had no way to return to the proper time.

Which meant they were stuck.

But was he thinking or planning on how he could survive the next hour? Or day?

Nope. His brain was utterly consumed by the revelation that Blayze was formally betrothed to another male.

Scowling in frustration, he watched as she gave a small shake of her head.

"My mother mentioned a betrothal, but I assumed that I was cursed before it could be formally announced."

"Who is the lucky male?"

"What does it matter?" she demanded in genuine confusion.

"I'm curious."

She paused as she searched her memory. Then she gave a faint shrug. "I believe his name was Bolt."

"Bolt," Char repeated, the name teasing at the edge of his mind.

"Do you know him?"

"The name is familiar." For some reason he felt a heaviness in his chest. As if the name was conjuring a dark memory. Then he had an abrupt vision of an ancient dragon with bent shoulders and an expression that was locked with sorrow. "Oh." He grimaced. "The son of Ash."

She studied him as if sensing the guilt that crawled through him, making him feel small and petty for his irrational jealousy.

"Is he a friend of yours?"

"Not Bolt," he said. "But I do remember Ash visiting my father's lair. It was always a somber event."

"I don't understand."

"I'm sorry, Blayze," he said, and he truly meant it. "Bolt was killed centuries ago."

She jerked, as if the words had hit her like a blow. "He's dead?"

"Yes."

"How?"

Char gave a slow shake of his head. He could remember hearing whispers of a sudden death. And that the details had been swept beneath the carpet. At the time, he'd been too young to really care what might have happened.

"No one spoke about it," he told Blayze.

"Why not?"

"I'm not sure," he admitted. "But you were right. It doesn't matter now."

And it didn't matter. Despite the fact that Bolt had mysteriously died, there would be another mate chosen for her. Well, assuming they didn't die before they could return to their time, there would be another mate chosen.

He sharply cut off the thought. What was wrong with him? He was never Mr. Doom and Gloom.

Dammit. They weren't going to die. Even if they couldn't leave this time. He was going to make sure of that. But first he needed to understand what had gone wrong.

He eased his grip on Blayze's arm and studied her upturned face. In the darkness her skin glowed with that soft luminance emphasizing her delicate beauty.

"I thought you said you followed the curse to bring us here?"

"I did."

He arched a brow. She had to have heard the conversation between the two female dragons who had just sashayed their way down the corridor.

"According to your father's guests, you haven't even been born yet," he pointed out. "Unless Synge has another daughter?"

She shook her head. "I was the only female."

"Then how did we get here?"

She wrinkled her slender nose. "My first thought was that I must have changed history by coming back through time."

Char grimaced. The fact that he had Dalia blood running through his veins meant that he was hauled kicking and screaming into every philosophical debate over the moral and magical conundrum of time travel.

It didn't matter that he could only slow time. And that he had no impact on the past or future. They always assumed he had some deep insight into the debate.

"You said that was your first thought," he said. "What about now?"

"Now I believe that I wasn't following the curse when I pulled on the strand of magic, but the original spell."

Char sighed. He thought her time travel theory was going to be confusing. Reversing magic was even worse.

"I don't understand."

"Neither do I," she murmured in soft tones. "Not yet."

"Blayze—" Char cut off his words as the sound of footsteps once again filled the air.

This time, however, it wasn't guests who were too preoccupied with their gossip to notice there was someone hidden in the storage closet.

Nope, it was a half-breed dragon who roughly jerked open the door to glare at them with blatant suspicion.

Char instinctively moved to stand in front of Blayze, protecting her from view. At the same time, he took a quick inventory of the male in front of him.

He was larger than Char and attired in the familiar uniform that marked him as one of Synge's guard. But Char was one of the few half-breeds who could actually shift into a dragon. Which meant he could destroy the male if necessary.

Of course, destroying fellow half-breeds was usually at the bottom of his to-do list. Unlike some of his more bloodthirsty friends, he preferred to charm his way out of a situation.

"What are you doing in here?" the male demanded.

Char flashed a smile even as his hand slipped behind his back. He never left home without his favorite dagger tucked into the sheath hidden at his lower back. It had been crafted deep in the bowels of the earth by orcs, and had a rare diamond blade. It was the only weapon that could slice through the thick scales of a dragon.

"Easy," Char murmured. "I can explain."

The guard scowled, but Char didn't miss the nervous way he clenched and unclenched his hands. He was young and obviously new to his position. The realization didn't ease Char's fears. There was nothing more dangerous than a twitchy servant hoping to impress his master.

As if to prove his point, the male pulled free his sword strapped to his side.

"You can explain it in the dungeons," he growled.

Char continued to smile, taking a step forward. His dagger was shorter than the sword. He needed any fight to be up close and personal. "No need for violence."

The male bristled, his eyes smoldering with fire. "I will decide what is needed."

Without warning, Char felt a stir of air as Blayze stepped to stand at his side. He turned his head to send her a warning glare, only to feel a stab of shock.

She looked different as she tilted her chin and smoothed her hands down the beaded gown that shimmered in the faint light. Her hair tumbled down her back in a river of ebony and her skin glowed liked the finest pearl.

She was more than beautiful. She was regal.

Majestic.

She was every inch a pureblooded dragon.

"Actually, I will be the one who decides," she announced in tones that defied argument.

The guard blinked, clearly dazzled by the glorious sight of Blayze. "Who are you?"

"I am a guest of Ravel."

The guard's lips parted, as if he was about to grill her for more details. Then he caught sight of her pale eyes that were sprinkled with pinpricks of color and his breath caught.

"You are from her clan," he said, the words more a statement than a question.

Obviously the eyes were a trait unique to Ravel's bloodline.

"I am," Blayze murmured.

Hastily shoving his sword back in its sheath, the guard performed a deep bow.

"Forgive me." He straightened, his gaze flicking to the cramped space behind them. "I did not expect to discover a guest in the storage closet."

Blayze sniffed. "I wished to have a word in private with my servant."

The guard frowned before he leaped to the most obvious conclusion. That Blayze had hidden in the closet so she could enjoy a quickie with her servant.

"I see," the male said.

Blayze gave another sniff and Char repressed a sudden urge to smile. She was remarkably good in her role as the arrogant, disdainful dragon.

"Doubtful."

The guard cleared his throat. It was unlikely his training included shooing guests and their servants out of the closets.

"Can I escort you to the throne room?" he at last offered.

Expecting her to demand that the guard leave them in peace, Char went rigid as she stepped forward.

"If you wish."

The guard backed away from the doorway and held out his arm. Blayze laid her fingers on the top of his wrist, allowing the male to escort her down the corridor.

Char swallowed his curse, hurrying forward. "Lady Blayze, perhaps we should finish our conversation," he growled in low tones.

She didn't even bother to glance in his direction. "Nonsense. We can speak later."

She swept forward, her spine straight and her shoulders squared.

Char forced himself to walk behind her, playing the role of the perfect servant. So much for his fierce determination to keep them alive.

They'd be lucky to survive the next hour.

CHAPTER SIX

Levet breathed out a tiny sigh of relief as the terrible tremors that were shaking The Viper Pit came to a halt.

He was hoping the sudden stillness was a sign that the magic that surrounded the building had entrapped the furious dragon. It was that or Synge was preparing to melt them with his dragon-fire.

Non. He would not consider the notion that he was about to be liquefied into a pile of goo. He'd discovered over the years that sticking his head in the sand was always a legitimate way to deal with a threat.

Beside him, the Anasso cocked his head to the side, no doubt trying to determine the threat level, while Viper was moving through the crowd below, trying to soothe the terrified demons.

"Shouldn't you go speak with Synge?" Levet prompted.

The oversized vampire turned his head to glare down at Levet.

"I have a better idea," he growled. "You go speak with him."

Levet took a hasty step backward, his tail twitching between his legs. He was not scared. But he was not the king. He was not even a prince. This was the sort of thing demons with big swords were supposed to take care of.

"Why should I go?" he demanded.

A frigid anger crackled through the air. "You're the one who told the dragons that vampires were responsible for his daughter's curse."

Levet clicked his tongue. Really, why was the male obsessed with that tiny, insignificant point?

"I told you. I simply shared what I discovered," he said.

There was the sound of footsteps before a large vampire dressed in black leather appeared on the balcony. One of the Ravens, Styx's personal bodyguards.

Styx moved to speak with the male, their voices too low for Levet to pick up the words. A few minutes later the vampire turned to leave and Levet moved to study Styx with a stab of impatience.

Every second that passed was another second that Synge might turn them all to toast.

"Well?" Levet prompted.

Styx's expression was grim. "Our protection spells are currently holding Synge in stasis, but it will only last a few hours."

Levet hid his expression of relief. No reason to reveal that he was going to use those few hours to get as far away from Chicago as possible. "What about Baine?"

Styx managed to look even more grim. An astonishing achievement.

"He's asking for an audience."

"Ah." Levet took another step back. "It appears you have the situation in hand—"

A squawk was wrenched from Levet's throat as Styx grasped the massive sword that was sheathed across his back and pulled it free. With one smooth motion he had the tip of the lethal weapon pressed against Levet's neck.

"This is your mess," the vampire informed Levet.

"Now you're going to fix it."

Levet's tail twitched, but he didn't move. The sword was sharp enough to chop off his head. The one certain way to kill a gargoyle.

"Moi?" He pretended he didn't notice the massive weapon jabbing into his thick hide. "It was a bloodsucker who was responsible. As the Anasso it is your responsibility to ensure they do not go about cursing dragons."

Ice crystals formed in the air as Styx leaned down, his power beating against Levet.

"Listen carefully, gargoyle."

Levet grimaced. "I do not like those words."

Styx ignored his grumbled complaint. "You are going to find the missing dragon."

Levet was momentarily confused. Then, he frowned as he realized who Styx meant.

"Blayze? How can I find her?"

"You claim to be a hero. Doesn't that include rescuing damsels in distress?" Styx demanded.

"Oui, but would it not make more sense to track down the vampire responsible for the curse?"

"What do you think is going to soothe a pissed-off dragon? The vampire who cursed his daughter? Or having that daughter back in his lair where he can protect her?"

Levet wrinkled his snout. It was true that if he managed to locate the vampire and hand him over to Synge, the dragon would torch him and remain pissed at the entire vampire race.

If he could find Blayze, the male might be distracted enough to return to his lair.

"Good point."

Styx straightened, lowering his sword. "You have eight hours."

"Or?"

Styx flashed his fangs. "Dragons will be the least of your concern."

Mon dieu.

CHAPTER SEVEN

Blayze was surprised how easy it was to assume the role of an arrogant, pureblooded dragon. Almost as if she was born to the role. And she supposed she was, despite the fact she'd been isolated her entire life.

She could only hope her brittle façade could last long enough for her to do a search of the lair.

Acutely aware of the heavy press of power that crackled and sizzled in the air as they reached the throne room, as well as Char's seething disapproval, she halted and removed her hand from the guard's arm.

"I can find my way now."

"My lady." The male offered a small bow before he was disappearing among the guests.

She dismissed him from her mind as she allowed her gaze to wander over the large room. It was remarkably plain, with woven rugs on the stone floor and torches stuck into the walls. At the far end was a high dais with two thrones. At the moment both of them were empty.

Her attention turned to the guests who were gathered in small clumps. Most of them were pureblooded dragons, although she could sense several fey creatures, as well as a few vampires.

Could one of them be responsible for her curse?

Taking a step forward, she abruptly felt her arm being grabbed in a tight grip as Char tugged her into a shadowed corner.

"What are you doing?" he hissed in frustration.

She reluctantly transferred her attention to the angry dragon standing in front of her. It wasn't just that she was in a hurry to search the room, but she'd discovered that it was almost impossible to concentrate on anything but Char when he was near.

How was a poor female supposed to think clearly when she was gazing at those pale, perfect features and the gray eyes that could appear as soft as smoke or harden to platinum? And how was she supposed to resist the urge to run her hands over his lean body so she could fully appreciate the steely strength of his muscles?

With an effort, she leashed her renegade reaction to the tempting male. She would fully explore her intense sexual awareness of Char once they weren't facing imminent death.

Her dragon huffed in protest.

Later, later, later…

"I'm attempting to locate the spell," she forced herself to say.

He paused, considering her explanation. "How can you find magic that hasn't been cast?"

The truth was that she hadn't entirely thought through her strategy. She only knew that she'd been brought to this point in time by the curse.

Surely that meant it was here?

"My mother always suspected that the curse had been created by a witch," she said.

Fewer than a handful of demons could actually create a curse with their own powers. More often than not, a demon was forced to seek out a witch who could create the curse and place it in a vessel until the caster was ready to release it.

Char blinked, looking suddenly hopeful. Witches were always human.

"If that's true, then it should be easy enough to spot a mortal. It's not like your father would invite a hundred of them to waltz through his throne room."

She wrinkled her nose. Like many other demon species, dragons had always harbored a deep distrust of humans in general, and witches in particular.

"It's doubtful the witch would be here," she admitted. "They more than likely bartered the spell to a dragon."

Char grimaced. "Do you think you can sense it?"

"That's my hope."

"And then?"

Her answer came without hesitation. "I will kill them."

The gray eyes flared with heat. Char clearly approved of her lust for blood.

The thought warmed her heart.

Char's fingers trailed up her arm, igniting sparks of pleasure. But before he could speak there was an oppressive sense of power that landed on top of them like a ton of bricks.

Blayze winced before she turned to face the dragon who was striding toward them with a suspicious expression. Damn. The guard had apparently left her to run and tattle to her father.

Now Synge was coming to demand explanations.

A large, brutish male with his dark hair shorn close to his head and eyes the color of polished pewter, he was an intimidating beast.

Instinctively, Blayze lowered her head and sank into a graceful curtsy. "My lord."

"My guard tells me that you are from my mate's clan," he said in blunt tones.

No one had ever accused Synge of being a diplomat.

"Yes." Straightening, Blayze lifted her head and met the older male's smoldering gaze.

Synge stilled, confusion rippling over his broad face as he caught sight of her unusual eyes. Then his nose flared as he tested her scent.

"Do I know you?" he demanded.

"I am Blayze," she said, remembering to keep her words formal. They had traveled backward in time, and the rules of etiquette were different.

Synge gave a slow shake of his head. "You seem familiar."

She offered a bland smile. She needed to get away from this male before he figured out why she seemed so familiar.

"I am here to celebrate the birth of your daughter."

Without warning the brutish features abruptly melted into an expression of deep, aching affection.

"My daughter," he breathed. "An unexpected blessing."

Blayze felt as if she'd just been slugged in the gut. How dare he act like he actually cared about his unborn child?

What game was he playing?

"Females are rare," she managed to say.

"She is a blessing because she carries the essence of my mate," he gruffly insisted, his gaze sweeping toward the female across the room.

Ravel was small for a pureblooded dragon, with delicate features. She had long, brilliant red hair and the same odd, opal eyes as Blayze. At the moment she was wearing a white silk gown that swept the floor and outlined her protruding stomach. She looked as if she was only minutes away from giving birth.

Blayze's heart twisted. Her mother had sacrificed everything to keep her alive. Including her own mate.

"I hope you keep them protected," she said before she could halt the words.

Heat scorched through the air, the ground trembling beneath her feet as her father stepped toward her.

"You have heard of a threat?"

"No," she hastily denied. "But there are always those who seek to harm a vulnerable hatchling. Even among our own people."

He scowled, like he was offended by the mere suggestion he might be less than diligent in protecting his family.

"Be assured that nothing will be allowed to harm my child. I will guard her with my life," he informed her in sharp tones.

Blayze hissed. The memory of how swiftly this male had turned his back on his precious child suddenly boiled through her blood.

He might mouth the words that claimed he would sacrifice his life for her, but as soon as she was cursed he'd been eager to toss her to the wolves. Or rather, he'd tossed her to the less than tender mercy of the Dragon Council, who'd condemned her to death.

"You—" Her words were cut short as Char reached out to give her arm a warning squeeze. She grimaced. Char was right. Venting her feelings would only put them in more danger. That was the last thing she wanted. "You are precisely the warrior I would desire to have at Ravel's side," she said in smooth tones.

Synge continued to frown, but seemingly accepting she wasn't a threat, he stepped back. "I must go," he said, swiveling on his heel to stride across the room.

Like a covey of nervous dew fairies, the guests scurried out of the way of the dragon who headed straight for the tiny, pregnant female across the room.

Blayze made a choked sound of disgust as she watched Synge place a protective arm around Ravel's slender shoulders. It was extremely rare for dragons to find a true mate. Most pairings were nothing more than political alliances meant to strengthen a clan.

But there was nothing political in the way Synge was gazing down at Ravel. Or how he reached to lay a gentle hand on her swollen belly.

"How is it possible?" Blayze rasped.

Char moved to stand beside her, his fingers stroking down her back. His touch was light, but it was enough to ease a portion of the anger that bubbled through her.

"How is what possible?" he asked.

Blayze nodded toward her parents. "How could he pretend he is so devoted to his unborn child?"

Char's fingers continued to move up and down her spine, the heat of his dragon wrapping around her in an unspoken cloak of comfort.

"I don't think he's pretending," he told her in soft tones.

She clenched her hands at her side, the pain of betrayal a hot knot of agony in the pit of her stomach. "A father who truly cares for his daughter doesn't allow her to be destroyed."

"Even if he believes it's what is best for you?" Char asked.

She sent him a disbelieving glare. "How could death be better?"

His fingers slid beneath her hair to cup her nape. Gently he massaged her rigid muscles. "He thought you were suffering."

She frowned. "He told you that?"

"No, but I spent several decades in this lair before I was given to Baine as his personal guard," he told her.

"And?"

Char turned his head, his gaze sweeping toward the couple across the room. The crowd of demons had moved to surround them, like a cluster of satellites caught in the gravitational force of a star. But Synge was large enough to tower over all of them.

"The Synge I know is a cold, brutal bastard who rules with fear and intimidation," Char said. "Until I witnessed him standing beside your bed after you'd been discovered alive, I would have sworn that he didn't possess a heart."

Blayze snorted. "He doesn't."

"Look at him, Blayze," Char urged in soft tones. "That isn't the expression of a male who doesn't care. It's the expression of a male who cares too much."

CHAPTER EIGHT

It had taken Levet less than five minutes to find a pretty imp who could open a portal so he could travel from Chicago to New York City.

Manhattan, to be more specific.

He sucked in a deep breath, catching the familiar combination of car exhaust, street food, and pure adrenaline.

There was no other place in the world like New York.

The narrow streets that were framed by towering buildings. The brilliant billboards flashing with a blinding explosion of color. The double-decker buses that belched out foul-smelling smoke.

Darting away from the public streets that were thickly crowded, Levet threaded his way between alleys until he was in a neighborhood that was never visited by the tourists.

When Styx had made his threat, Levet's first impulse had been to disappear for the next few centuries. Not even a vampire could hold a grudge forever, could he?

But even as the large vampire had stalked away to speak with Baine, Levet had been struck by a crazy notion.

After breaking the illusion in Blayze's private chamber, he hadn't sensed any intruder. Which meant he didn't have the skills to discover who had taken her, or where they might be now.

But there might be someone who could help.

Reaching a narrow brick building that looked abandoned to anyone passing by, Levet allowed a smile of relief to touch his lips. Even from a distance, he could feel the magic that pulsed in the air.

The club was still there.

Crossing the dark street, he laid his palm against the spell that surrounded the shabby building. A second later it began to pulse and crack. Enchantment sprinkled the air, rich with the scent of warm honey. Then, without warning, the sidewalk shuddered and the illusion shattered.

The decrepit dump was gone, and in its place was an elegant structure that looked like a Grecian villa with lots of white marble, fluted columns and tall windows. Levet waddled up the narrow flight of stairs and knocked on one of the double doors.

On cue, a small panel in the door slid open and a gruff voice floated through the air. "Levet?"

"Oui." Levet spread his arms wide. "'Tis the world-famous Levet."

"About damned time," the unseen demon muttered.

Levet gave a flutter of his wings. It was always a pleasure to be appreciated by the lesser—

"Eek." He released a small shriek as one of the

doors was jerked open and a hand reached out to grab him by the horn.

With a blur of motion, he was pulled into the public room of the club.

A quick glance revealed a long, sunken room with white marble floors and glass walls that reflected the crowd of demons that filled the tables. Above his head, the ceiling was sparkling with tiny, magical butterflies that glittered over the dance floor below them.

For a demon bar it was astonishingly elegant. Classy.

Vampires tended to be civilized, but the other demon species remained barbarians. Usually they gathered in holes in the ground that were filled with drunken trolls and fighting cages. This place catered to guests that avoided most other clubs.

Harpies. Pixies. And even a few human witches.

The combination sizzled with emotions, as if the crowd that filled the room was electrifying the very air.

Levet returned his attention to the demon who had so rudely snatched him off the front step.

The creature was a mongrel, with a mishmash of ancestors. There was some troll blood that had allowed him to grow over seven feet tall with heavy features that included a protruding brow, a lower jaw that jutted out with a set of curved fangs. But his pale, hairless skin suggested he had some orc blood mingled in. Probably a bit of fairy in there somewhere as well.

He was unique enough that Levet instantly recognized him.

"Oh, it is you, Crowley," he said, his tail twitching as the demon continued to hold him off the ground. Really, why were demons forever grabbing his horns? It was as if they had some strange fetish. "What a lovely surprise," he continued, a smile pasted to his lips. "Is that a new tumor on your neck? It is quite stylish."

"I've been looking for you," Crowley snarled, his eyes glowing red.

"For *moi*? How nice."

"It's nice for me. Now I don't have to worry about trying to hunt you down," Crowley said, his protruding lower jaw making the words come out slurred.

Levet's smile never faltered. "You do know that most demons find that the chase is much more entertaining than capturing your prize?"

"Nothing will be more entertaining than ripping out your heart and eating it."

He lifted Levet even higher.

As if he was judging whether he could eat him in one bite.

"No need for haste, Crowley."

The demon pulled back his lips, revealing his razor-sharp teeth. "Don't worry. I intend to take my time."

"If this is about your daughter—"

Crowley released a deafening roar that sent the nearby pixies diving beneath their tables and the butterflies zigzagging in a dizzying circle, like a strobe light the humans used in their clubs.

Levet grimaced. It'd been two centuries since Levet had met Crowley's daughter at a tribal gathering in Siberia. It was not his fault that the awkward young female had developed a violent crush on him and tried to follow him back to America.

He was quite simply irresistible to women.

Crowley's flat nose flared with fury. "I am going to smoosh you."

"Smoosh me?" Levet clicked his tongue. He had been insulted and badgered by the very best. This demon was a sad disappointment. "Troll mongrels are as tedious as full-blooded trolls. If you are going to threaten me, you could at least come up with something more clever."

Crowley tilted back his head to bray like a mule.

Levet assumed it was the mongrel's version of a hissy fit.

Before he could do any smooshing, however, a rich, throaty voice echoed through the club, brushing over Levet's skin like black velvet.

"Release him, Crowley."

Levet swiveled his head in time to watch a female step out of a door near the back of the club.

She was a tiny wisp of a creature with a heart-shaped face and golden eyes that held flecks of starlight. Her hair was inky black and cut so short it should have made her look like a boy. But there was nothing boyish about her. Not even with the leather pants and heavy boots that she wore.

Maybe it was the red, sparkly halter that molded to her firm breasts. Or the sway of her hips as she strolled toward him. Or, more likely, it was the feminine power that burned around her with tangible force.

No one could mistake her for anything but a fiercely dangerous female.

Levet smiled. He'd met Vex in Greece shortly after he'd been kicked out of the Gargoyle Guild. She'd been tossed out of the Succubus Guild about the same time. It was only natural that the two outcasts would form a friendship that had lasted over the centuries.

"*Oui*, Crowley, release me," he said to the demon who continued to dangle him by the horn.

Crowley growled, curling back his lips as if about to take a bite. Then power zapped through the room, silencing the guests and making the troll mongrel give a small whimper. Vex had the ability to enter a person's mind and do all sorts of bad, bad things.

"Crowley, I said release him."

The troll mongrel dropped Levet to the ground and scurried away with his stunted tail between his legs.

Levet flapped his wings as Vex strolled to stand at

his side. She topped him by several inches, but she was one of the few demons who didn't tower over him.

"Still making friends wherever you go, eh Levet?"

Levet gave a lift of his hands. "But of course. I am adorable."

"Hmm." Her lips twitched. "What are you doing here? The last I heard, you were too good for the rest of us riffraff. Aren't you rubbing elbows with royalty now?"

Levet puffed out his chest. "It is true my services are in high demand with the most powerful demons."

"So what brings you to the gutters?"

Levet snorted, glancing around the large room filled with marble, crystal and drunken guests.

"As a demon who has spent many years in the gutters, as well as the sewers, and several moldy crypts, I can assure you this fine establishment does not resemble any of those nasty locations," he said.

Vex shrugged. She was well aware that an invitation to her private club was a privilege that demons often fought over.

"Let's get a drink," she said, turning to lead him across the dance floor. Instantly the crowd scurried to get out of her path. She might be small, but there was no doubt that Vex was queen of her domain. "I have a private stash of nectar in my office."

Levet waited until they'd entered the long room that looked more suited for a human professor. The walls were hidden behind shelves stuffed with leather-bound books, and woven carpets covered the floor. At the far end a massive desk was situated near a fireplace.

"You may not feel so generous with your nectar when you discover why I am here," Levet warned, watching the slender succubus as she poured a thick, amber liquid into two fluted glasses.

Vex turned to thrust a glass into his hand before she

leaned against the edge of the desk. "Are you in trouble?"

Levet sipped the nectar, his tail twitching as the fey magic warmed his blood.

"It was not my fault," he assured his companion.

Vex rolled her eyes. "It never is. Not even when you dared that Baon demon to try and sneak into the orc nest to steal his demon brew."

Levet tried to look innocent. Baon was a slough demon who was terrorizing a tribe of wood nymphs when Levet and Vex happened to be passing through. Levet challenged the idiot to see who could steal the demon brew the quickest.

"How could I know that he was protected by a pack of hellhounds?"

Vex chuckled. "The last I saw of the demon he was running down the side of the mountain with at least two hellhounds biting his ass. I bet he couldn't sit for a month."

"It could not have happened to a better demon," Levet said.

"True." Vex held her glass up in a mocking toast before tossing back the nectar in one gulp. She licked her full lips as she set aside the empty glass on the desk and regarded Levet with a searching gaze. "Now, tell me what you need from me."

Levet continued to savor the nectar in small sips. Unlike Vex, he didn't have the money or clout to get his hands on the rare drink.

Between swallows, Levet recounted the events over the past few days, including Torque's mating with Rya and how they'd located Synge's daughter, Blayze. Then he told her about his journey to Synge's lair where he'd broken through the illusion to reveal the echoes of the curse, and the fact that it'd been released by a vampire.

When he was done, he studied Vex's pale, perfect

face. The last thing he expected was for her to tilt back her head and chuckle with rich amusement.

"There's a pissed-off dragon trapped on the top of The Viper Pit?"

Levet swallowed a sigh. He'd forgotten that Viper and Vex had a less-than-friendly competition between their rival nightclubs.

"Unfortunately, Styx does not find it nearly so amusing," he muttered.

"He wouldn't," she said in dry tones. "I'm afraid I don't have any skill that would help kill a dragon." She pretended to consider for a long moment. "Of course, if you're hoping to kill the vampires I might be able to hook you up."

Levet gave a hasty shake of his head. "No killing."

Vex wrinkled her nose. "You didn't use to be such a party pooper."

"I am not a poop of the party," Levet denied. "I merely wish to prevent a war between the dragons and vampires. It would make my friend Tayla most unhappy."

Vex folded her arms over her chest. "It would make the entire demon world unhappy. War is always messy. And if it is between two of the most fierce predators…"

A hush filled the office as they both contemplated the horror.

It was Levet who at last broke the silence. "I need to find Blayze and return her to Synge's lair before that happens," he told his companion. "Will you help?"

She gave a slow nod. "Take me to where your dragon disappeared."

CHAPTER NINE

As much as Char wanted to toss Blayze over his shoulder and carry her out of the throne room, he was smart enough to comprehend her fierce need to discover who'd hated her enough to curse her. And to relish her long overdue desire for revenge.

Leashing his dragon instincts, he took a position behind Blayze as she slowly began to weave her way through the guests. Most of them ignored her as they concentrated on trying to find the best position to be seen by Synge. No doubt they hoped to attract the attention of the powerful dragon to barter for some favor.

Char had witnessed the same behavior during the centuries he'd spent standing beside Baine. Dragons never gathered together simply to have a good time and enjoy each other's company. It was all about angling for greater power and riches to add to their hoard.

Kind of sad, when he thought about it.

Char gave a shake of his head. Now wasn't the time to regret the dragons' lack of social skills.

If Blayze's theory was right, somewhere in this room was a craven bastard who was willing to curse a mere babe. He needed to focus on keeping her safe. Plus, he didn't like the way the male gazes were following her slender body as she moved through the room with her shimmering beaded gown and luminous skin.

His dragon stirred inside him, restless to warn off the idiots who dared to even glance in her direction.

In an effort to keep himself from doing something stupid, he moved to walk close beside Blayze.

"Do you sense anything?" he demanded.

She gave a small shake of her head. "Not yet."

His lips parted, but before he could continue the conversation, his attention was captured by the sight of two male dragons huddled together, whispering in the shadows.

One was almost as large as Synge, although not as muscular, with long black hair and a heavily jowled face. He was wearing a long crimson robe that was threaded with gold and decorated with large diamonds around the collar. His companion was smaller, with the same dark hair and dark eyes. He was wearing a similar robe, although it lacked the sparkle factor.

He looked like the dragon version of a Mini-Me.

Char's gaze narrowed as the two dragons began to inch along the edge of the crowd, clearly headed toward the nearby door.

He reached to lightly touch Blayze's arm. "Wait," he murmured.

She turned her head, her face unreadable. "What is it?"

"You continue to mingle," he told her.

"What about you?"

Char gave a covert nod of his head toward the dragons who'd captured his attention.

"Those two are looking pretty shady," he said in low tones. "I want to find out what's going on."

She gave a slow nod of her head. "Fine."

His fingers tightened on her arm. "While I'm gone, don't leave this room."

She blinked, her head tilting to the side. "Why do you assume you can give me orders?" Her tone was more curious than angry.

"Because I was given the duty of protecting you." He gazed down at her upturned face. When had he memorized each sweep and curve of her features? The wide brow. The slender nose. The high slashes of her cheekbones. The plush temptation of her lips. Probably the second he'd caught sight of her lying helpless on her bed. "There's no way in hell I'm going to let anything happen to you."

Her brows drew together. As if she was troubled by his response, but she wasn't sure why.

"I'm a duty?" she demanded.

Char released a short laugh. "That's what I'm trying to convince myself."

She continued to look puzzled. "That doesn't make any sense."

"I'm painfully aware of that," he muttered, shaking his head as he released her arm and stepped back. "Don't leave this room."

He didn't give her the opportunity to respond. Instead he plunged into the milling crowd, ignoring the furious glares as he elbowed his way to the far wall.

He didn't want the two dragons to disappear among the maze of corridors that crisscrossed the lair.

Stepping out of the throne room, he paused long enough to determine the echo of footsteps was coming from his left. He pressed close to the wall as he followed the fading sound.

The lair wasn't exactly the same as it would be in the future, but it was close enough for Char to realize they were headed toward the harem. He could already catch the rich scent of perfumed oils in the air.

He grimaced. Was it possible the two dragons were simply going to indulge their passions? It was hardly unusual for party guests to seek out companionship among the female servants.

He hesitated at the arched opening to the harem, peeking a glance into the large inner chamber.

The floor was covered with mosaic tiles, and in the center was a large fountain that sprayed water into the air. The walls were made of delicate latticework, and the ceiling was domed and covered with precious gems.

Char watched as the two males crossed the floor, waving away the females who scurried to offer their services. They exited into a darkened room on the other side of the main chamber.

Char shuffled through his memories. When he'd been living in this lair, that particular room the males had just entered was one of the few spaces that had only one entrance. Which meant no one could easily creep up to overhear their conversation.

Thankfully, his time in this household meant he was well aware that Synge was deeply suspicious of anyone who entered his lair. The ancient dragon had dozens of hidden tunnels that threaded their way between the various chambers.

A perfect place to listen in to private exchanges.

His brow furrowed as he tried to recall where the opening to the nearest tunnel was located. At the same time, he caught the scent of cherries as a pretty imp crossed the harem floor to peer out the door.

She had golden curls that tumbled down her back, a pale face that was dominated by a pair of green eyes, and a lush figure that was put on full display by the sheer gown that hugged her curves.

Exactly the sort of female who should have had him panting with appreciation.

Instead, he was trying to figure out how to get rid of her so he could continue with his quest.

"Do you seek entertainment?" the imp asked, her gaze taking a slow, appreciative survey of Char.

He silently formed a dozen different lies. Then he abruptly dismissed them.

Servants were far more observant than most purebloods ever realized. The female could be an asset if he could convince her that he wasn't there to harm Synge or his family.

"No, I seek a means to overhear a private conversation," he confessed in a soft voice, his gaze moving toward the door that was firmly closing behind the two dragons.

She stiffened, assuming an air of outrage. "Servants do not spy on guests in this lair."

Char flattened his lips, hiding his smile. He doubted that things had changed so drastically from century to century. Servants *always* spied on the guests. Then they would pass along any juicy gossip to Synge knowing that they would be well rewarded.

"Of course not," he quickly agreed. "But I am a personal guard within Ravel's clan. We believe she and the child she is carrying might be in danger."

A sincere concern rippled over the pale, lovely face. It seemed that Ravel was popular among the servants.

"Have you informed the master?" she demanded.

He heaved a rueful sigh. "I did try. Unfortunately, he is convinced no one would dare harm his mate." Char held the imp's gaze. "I cannot entirely share his confidence."

The imp bit her bottom lip, clearly torn between her

loyalty to Synge and her worry that something might happen to Ravel. At last she squared her shoulders. Her decision was made.

"Do you swear never to reveal I assisted you?" she asked.

He pressed a hand to the center of his chest. "I swear."

With a glance over her shoulder to make sure the two males were still behind the closed door, she stepped into the corridor with him.

"This way," she said, leading him a short distance to an elaborate tapestry that was hung on the stone wall.

Pulling it back, she revealed a narrow opening that ran between the rooms.

"Thank you," Char murmured, stepping toward the opening.

Without warning the imp leaned forward, trailing her fingers lightly down Char's neck.

"If you wish to thank me, I have a perfect means," she said in husky tones. "I will be waiting in the harem when you have finished your business."

Char found himself oddly tongue-tied. Where was his quick wit? He was a master of flirtation. Or at least he used to be.

Right now he felt as awkward as a bashful troll.

"I—"

The imp dropped her hand and stepped back. "You are mated?"

Mated. The word hung in the air like a hand grenade that might explode at any second.

Then, like any male who was contemplating having his entire world turned upside down, he cowardly slammed the mental door on the mere notion. Much better to pretend he didn't know what was going on.

"I am not certain what I am," he told her.

She heaved a deep sigh. "A shame."

"No shit."

With a shake of his head, Char hurried down the narrow space. His strange fascination with Blayze was a distraction he didn't need. Not now.

Probably not ever.

He slowed and came to a halt as the sound of male voices floated through a trellised grate just ahead. He wanted to get closer, but he didn't dare take the risk they could sense his presence. Right now his scent could easily be coming from any of the nearby rooms.

Turning so he could place his back against the wall and prevent anyone from sneaking up on him, Char concentrated on the low conversation.

"Do you have confirmation?" one of the dragons was asking. Char was guessing it was the smaller dragon. His voice held a note of ass-kissing that meant he was the weaker of the two.

In dragons, size really did matter.

"Yes. Ash confessed that he had agreed to a betrothal between his oldest son Bolt and Synge's unborn daughter," a deeper, rougher voice answered.

"A certain maneuver for power."

"Undoubtedly." There was the sound of footsteps, as if the larger dragon was pacing from one end of the room to the other. "Logic would demand he challenge me for my seat on the Council. I am in the weakest position."

"I have heard rumors that Synge has quietly started to return the bulk of his warriors to the lair."

Char grimaced as a blast of heat managed to sear through the wall. The dragon might be the weakest member of the Council, but that meant he was still mightier than ninety-nine percent of all other dragons.

"That's what I feared," he growled. "Synge will make his challenge as soon as the babe is born."

"You are certain it will not be before?"

"Ash is a cautious dragon. He will not complete the betrothal contract until the baby is born and pronounced an untainted pureblood."

Char arched a brow. He'd never heard that babies were tested for the purity of their blood. It had to be a secret dragon thing that wasn't shared with half-breeds like him.

"You should strike now," the first dragon encouraged.

"No." More heat blasted through the air. Char felt sweat dripping down his spine. "If there is an attempt to kill Synge or Ravel the blame will naturally be placed on me."

"True." There was a short pause. "So what is your plan?"

"I intend to destroy any hope of Synge using his daughter as a bargaining tool to empower his clan. Indeed, I hope I can crush any ambition he might harbor."

"How?"

The larger dragon chuckled. The sound echoed eerily through the narrow space where Char was hiding.

"The seed of my destruction has just arrived," he said.

Seed of destruction? Char would have laughed at the melodramatic words if he wasn't struck by a sudden fear.

The bastard had to be talking about the curse. What better means of wounding Synge than forcing him to agree to a death sentence for his only daughter?

It was cunning. And utterly evil.

"Where?" the lesser dragon demanded.

"The servants' quarters."

"How…" The dragon's words trailed away. "Ah. He is a member of Synge's household staff?"

Another creepy-ass chuckle. "A trusted member."

"You are a devious dragon, Magma."

"Which is why I am a member of the Council. And why I will remain a member," the larger dragon declared in harsh tones. "Now we need to return to the gathering. I cannot risk attracting attention by my absence."

There was the sound of footsteps, then a door opening and closing. Char barely noticed. Instead he was tucking the name Magma into the back of his mind. He was going to hunt the dragon down and kill him, he silently promised himself

He didn't know how. Not yet. But it was going to happen.

But first he had to discover the identity of the treacherous servant who intended to curse Blayze.

***

Levet used his mental connection with Tayla to request a portal to Synge's lair.

Seconds later, he was stepping out of the gateway along with Vex to discover the golden-haired imp standing at the opening to the lair with a worried expression.

"Vex, this is Tayla." He made the introduction with a wave of his hand.

Tayla offered the succubus a strained smile. "Thank you so much for agreeing to help."

Vex shrugged. "I owe Levet," she said. "He rescued me from a pack of hobgoblins who were planning to sell me to the slavers."

Tayla sent Levet a fond glance. "We all owe Levet," she murmured in soft tones. Levet preened. It was true. He was a hero to countless females. But before he could fully savor the praise, Tayla was turning her attention to the reason that Vex was there. "Is there anything I can do?"

"I need something that can connect me with the missing dragon," Vex told her.

Tayla stepped back, waving them into the lair. "This way."

They moved through the web of corridors, the silence in the lair an oppressive force. No doubt everyone was busy preparing for war.

Not the most pleasant thought.

Disturbed by the ominous atmosphere, it took several minutes for Levet to finally notice Vex's rigid tension as she walked beside him.

He frowned. Vex had been quick to agree to his request for her assistance. But now he sensed that she was regretting her choice.

"Is something wrong, *ma belle*?" he asked.

Vex wrapped her arms around her waist as a shiver shook her body. "It has been a long time since I was in a dragon's lair."

Levet arched his brows. "I did not know you were ever in one."

She hunched a shoulder, her golden eyes dark with an ancient pain. "My mother bartered me to a harem when I was kicked out of the Guild."

Tayla glanced over her shoulder with a sympathetic expression. "Why would your mother kick you out of the Guild?"

"Because I'm a succubus who doesn't feed on or control others with sex," Vex admitted.

Tayla blinked. "Then how do you feed?"

"I can absorb mental energy."

Tayla looked predictably confused, but before Vex could answer, Levet jumped into the conversation.

"You should see her. *Mon dieu*, it is magnificent. She can go into a demon's mind and suck up all the buzzy stuff."

Tayla blinked. "Buzzy stuff?"

Levet waved his hand. "You know, the energy that zaps through our heads. And when she is in there she can control a creature's mind."

Tayla glanced toward Vex. "Is that true?"

Vex nodded. "Pretty much. I feed on the electricity that is generated by a demon's brain, and I can use my powers to control that demon's mind for a limited time."

"So you're a cerebral succubus," Tayla said.

Vex looked momentarily shocked, as if she'd never thought about her gift in those terms. Then without warning she tilted back her head to release a deep belly laugh.

"I suppose that's true," Vex agreed, a portion of her tension easing.

They turned into the corridor that led to Synge's private quarters. Torches flickered, revealing the elaborate tapestries that hung on the walls.

"How did you escape the harem?" Levet demanded.

The warm scent of cherries spiced the air. "A male dragon bought my contract and released me."

Levet sent Vex a startled glance. Dragons weren't known for their generous natures. If a male used a part of his precious hoard to buy a beautiful female, it wasn't just to release her.

That was how Tayla had ended up a prisoner to Baine, although she now claimed that she was happy to be his slave. Or mate, as she preferred to be called.

A pity. But not every creature could have the exquisite taste to choose a gargoyle as their lover.

"Did you barter for your freedom?" he asked Vex.

Color touched her cheeks. Was she blushing?

"He offered to claim me as his mate."

Levet widened his eyes in shock. "You are mated to a dragon?"

She gave a slow shake of her head. "No. He disappeared before we could complete the mating."

Levet sensed the deep sadness that always lurked beneath Vex's kick-ass exterior. He had assumed that it was because she had been evicted from the Guild. He knew from painful experience that it was a wound that never truly healed. But now he realized that she'd had more than one betrayal in her life.

"How does a dragon disappear?" he demanded.

Vex's features abruptly hardened, but she couldn't disguise her lingering pain. "He clearly decided that I was unworthy."

Levet reached out to lightly touch her arm. "You are more worthy than any stupid dragon. Do not let the idiot make you turquoise."

Vex forced a smile to her lips. "Blue. Make you blue."

Levet wrinkled his snout. "Turquoise is blue, is it not?"

Tayla interrupted their conversation as she pulled open a heavy door and ushered them into the bedchamber.

"This is where Blayze was last seen," the imp said, pointing toward the bed. "She was lying there."

Vex nodded, moving forward to perch on the edge of the bed.

"Okay," she said. "Let's do this."

CHAPTER TEN

Char paused to smooth the short strands of his hair and to ensure that there was no dust clinging to his clothing before he returned to the throne room. Then he forced himself to count to one hundred.

He'd learned from a young age that dragons missed nothing. Even if they acted like they were entirely focused on Synge and his mate, Ravel, not one of them was blind to what was happening in the room behind them.

Including the fact that Magma had disappeared and recently returned.

The last thing he wanted was the dragon's return to be associated with his own.

Finally, he casually strolled through the doorway and along the edge of the crowd. He kept his gaze lowered as was expected for a mere half-breed, and used his sense of smell to direct him to Blayze.

Not that he actually needed her scent.

There was something deep inside him that would always pull him to her side. Like a homing pigeon.

A terrifying realization—that was tucked in the back of his head along with all the other terrifying realizations. Eventually they were going to cause a blockage in his brain, but until then he could pretend he didn't know they were there.

Halting next to Blayze, he offered a proper nod of his head.

Not that Blayze was equally discreet. Instead of treating him with the appropriate disdain that most dragons offered their servants, she reached to grasp his forearm, pulling him closer.

"You discovered something," she said, the words more a statement than a question.

Char grimaced. "So much for my poker face."

She furrowed her brow. "Poker face?"

"Never mind."

"What did you learn?" she pressed.

Char cast a covert glance around the swelling crowd. It seemed impossible to believe that they could stuff additional guests in the room without the floor collapsing.

There was no way to speak without someone overhearing them. Plus, the air was becoming uncomfortably hot. A danger when you had too many dragons squashed into the same space.

"Let's get a breath of fresh air."

Her lips parted, as if she was going to demand an immediate explanation. Then, seeming to realize there was no way to have a private conversation surrounded by so many demons, she gave a small nod. "We can return to my nursery."

He allowed her to usher him from the room, his head once again lowered as they left the throne room and walked down the corridor. He remained silent until they at last entered the room where they'd first arrived. He hadn't forgotten how easily they'd overheard the conversations between the two female dragons who'd been walking down this same hallway.

Once inside the room, he shut the door and headed toward the back wall.

"What are you doing?" Blayze demanded.

"I need to make sure there aren't any tunnels behind the walls."

"There's no need," she assured him.

He turned, his heart skipping a beat as he caught sight of her luminous glow in the dark room. *By the goddess.* She was so lovely. Like an angel.

Well, an angel who could breathe fire and kick the ass of nearly every other demon in the universe.

"How can you be sure?" he asked.

She waved a hand. "Just beyond this room is my father's hoard."

He was about to point out that his hoard might have been in a different area of the lair during this time period, only to snap his lips shut. Now that he actually paid attention to his surroundings, he could feel the heavy throb of magic that pulsed through the air. It was far enough away that it wasn't an in-your-face punch of power, but he sensed he wouldn't have to walk very far down the corridor to hit a wall of magic.

"No wonder your father chose this spot for your nursery," he said, crossing the floor to stand in front of Blayze. His hand reached to brush a strand of her ebony hair behind her ear. "He must have assumed that it was the safest place in the entire lair."

She stilled, her eyes vibrant with pinpricks of color. Heat seared through the air, sizzling over Char's skin. At the same time the scent of exotic spices teased at his nose. But even as his gaze dropped to the plush temptation of her lips, she was taking a tiny step backward.

"Tell me what you discovered," she said.

Char clenched his teeth. His dragon roared deep inside him. It was becoming almost impossible to keep his beast restrained. Only the knowledge that Blayze's enemies were lurking just beyond the closed door allowed him to battle through the sharp-edged hunger that threatened to cloud his mind.

That and the knowledge that Synge would roast him alive if he discovered that Char was aching to kiss her from the top of her head to the tips of her tiny toes.

"The dragons I followed are plotting against your father," he finally managed to say.

"Why?"

"Because Magma fears that Synge intends to challenge him for his seat on the Council."

She gave a slow nod, as if she'd already suspected what he was going to say.

"Do you recognize Magma?" she asked.

"No. I had limited contact with the Dragon Council. When I was in the service of my father, and then Synge, I was kept in the servants' quarters," he said. "And after I was sent to Baine we spent most of our time searching the various dimensions for rare manuscripts. He had no interest in the constant power struggles between dragon clans."

Baine's lack of ambition had been shocking to Char, who'd been sired by a dragon who lusted after power. And it'd taken Char several years to truly believe that Baine was more interested in learning than collecting a vast hoard.

Over the centuries, however, Char had developed a deep respect for his master's cunning. Baine might not seek power or riches, but his vast knowledge of the various worlds and the creatures that inhabited them made him a formidable adversary.

"What does Magma intend to do to my father?" Blayze asked.

"Not your father." He held her gaze. "You."

She stiffened. "The curse."

Char grimaced. "He didn't say it in those words, but he made it clear that he intended to distract your father by hurting his daughter as soon as she was born."

Her jaw clenched, but there wasn't any hint of fear on her beautiful face. Instead, her features hardened as she abruptly pivoted on her heel. "Then I'll kill him."

Char reached out to grasp her arm, gently turning her back to face him.

"Hold on, sweetheart," he murmured.

She blinked. "Sweetheart?"

He ignored her surprise at the endearment. What could he say? That he wanted to call her *sweetheart*, and *baby*, and *darling*, and all those other silly names that he used to make fun of males for saying?

"First we need to find the servant who has the curse," he said, well aware that his words would distract her.

He was right.

She was instantly focused on his revelation. "Magma used his servant to bring the curse into the lair?"

"Not one of his servants," he corrected. "He used one of your father's servants."

Her eyes widened, her breath hissing between her clenched teeth. "That's why my mother couldn't discover who was responsible. No one would suspect that it could be a member of my father's household. Not when they must know that he would destroy them if he discovered the truth." She gave a disbelieving shake of her head. It was rare to find anyone stupid enough to betray a pureblood dragon. "We need to get to the servants' quarters."

Char scowled. "Not we." His fingers tightened on her arm. "Me."

She narrowed her opal eyes. "Can you sense the curse?"

"No, but I can…" He considered the proper word. Torture. Rampage. Brutalize. "*Encourage* the servants to tell me who the traitor is."

She snorted. "My way is faster."

He shrugged. He couldn't argue, but that didn't mean he was going to allow her to waltz into danger. "My way is safer."

Her expression tensed. Not with anger. But with something that was perilously close to disappointment.

"My mother nearly smothered me with her need to protect me," she said in soft tones. "I won't be caged again."

His heart dropped to his toes. He had a vivid memory of walking into this precise room when Synge had commanded he protect his daughter.

Blayze had been lying unconscious on the bed, wrapped in magic that was meant to protect her. She'd been pale, and as still as death. A prisoner in her own mind.

It was an image he never, ever wanted to see again.

He heaved an unsteady sigh. "You're killing me," he muttered.

She reached up to lightly touch his face. "I'm sorry."

It was her touch that did it.

He'd been behaving. Hell, he'd practically been a saint. What other dragon could have resisted the urge to strip off her sparkly gown and breathe fire over her luminous flesh?

Now his hands reached to cup her face as his head lowered. He pressed his lips against her soft mouth.

Passion blasted through him. Immediate, white-hot and shockingly vast.

Her lips were lush and soft and spiced with sweet temptation. The taste flooded his senses, as intoxicating as demon's brew.

There was a rustle of silk as she stepped closer, allowing the heat of her dragon to play over his body. Char groaned, his fingers skimming down the side of her neck.

Her skin glowed brighter, her eyes shimmering with breathtaking beauty. The sight ignited his flames, and they danced around them as his dragon snarled in an effort to be let free.

Danger. Danger. Danger.

The word whispered in the back of his mind, and with a muttered curse, he forced himself to pull away.

"Let's go," he rasped.

He continued to play with fire. Literally.

One of these times, he was going to get burned.

CHAPTER ELEVEN

Blayze felt dizzy. Or maybe she was giddy.

Hard to tell, since she had zero actual experience with desire.

What she did know was that the quicker she could kill the treacherous servant who intended to curse her, the quicker she could drag Char into a private room and lock the door.

She wanted to fully explore the sensations that were scorching through her body. And she wanted to make sure that the next time Char kissed her there was nothing to stop him from continuing with his seduction.

Or maybe she would seduce him.

It couldn't be that hard to figure out, could it?

The warm giddiness continued to flow through her body as Char steered her down a separate hallway that led away from the more formal area of the lair. It felt glorious, or at least it did until she noticed the tension that was humming around Char as he walked beside her.

Turning her head, she met his brooding gaze. "Is something wrong?"

He paused before abruptly speaking. "Am I the first?"

She blinked, not entirely sure what he was asking. "What do you mean?"

"Am I the first male to kiss you?"

"Oh." She blinked in surprise. It was a strange question, considering that he had to know she'd been cursed when she was just a hatchling. "Yes, you're the first."

Another brooding glance. "Are you sorry?"

"Why would I be sorry?"

His hands balled into fists, as if he was struggling to contain some fierce emotion.

"You've pointed out that I'm a half-breed more than once."

She frowned. She'd pointed out he was a half-breed because he *was* a half-breed. Why would that bother him?

It took several seconds before she at last realized that he'd mistakenly assumed she considered his mixed heritage to be a bad thing.

She came to a halt. She could already catch the scent of fairies and vampires and even goblins that seeped through the air. Which meant the servants' quarters was just ahead.

Right now, however, she was more interested in Char's idiotic belief that she cared about his pedigree.

"I've spent centuries locked away from the world," she reminded him. "It allowed me to concentrate on what was important. And what was stupid."

His studied her face, as if searching for some hidden meaning in her words. "So what's important?"

She didn't even have to think about it. "Loyalty.

Trust. Devotion."

Fire briefly danced over his skin. Blayze's heart missed a beat at the beauty of the silvery flames.

"Yes," he breathed.

She smiled. She liked the dazed look on his face. Just as much as she liked the knowledge that she'd put it there.

She tilted her head to the side, sending him a coy glance. Or at least she hoped it was coy. She might just look ridiculous.

"You didn't ask what I thought was stupid," she told him.

His eyes smoldered, the flames continuing to halo his body. "I'm afraid."

She allowed her fingers to brush up his arm, savoring the feel of his dragon-fire.

"I think it's stupid to waste your days pursuing power and riches." She answered the question he refused to ask. "Or judging others by the purity of their blood rather than the contents of their heart."

Something in his expression seemed to ease, as if a weight was lifted off his shoulders. Still, he studied her with a wary gaze.

"I doubt your parents would agree."

Blayze shrugged. She would always owe her mother a huge debt. The female dragon had sacrificed everything to keep Blayze protected. But while she loved her mother, she was done having her life controlled by others.

From now on, she was living each day precisely as she wanted to.

"Thank the goddess I am finally allowed to make my own decisions."

His fingers brushed over her lips, but he didn't lean down and kiss her as she hoped. Instead, he drew in a deep breath, and turned to continue down the corridor.

"We'll finish this conversation after we find the servant and destroy the curse."

Blayze shrugged and fell into step beside him. She didn't understand why he was so suspicious. Did he expect her to change her mind? She'd had centuries to witness the world, even if it was through her mother's eyes. She knew what she wanted for her future.

And Char was becoming more firmly woven into her plans.

Unless…Blayze frowned as she was struck by a sudden thought.

"What about you?" she abruptly demanded.

He glanced down at her in confusion. "What are you asking?"

"You are a servant to Baine."

He nodded. "I am."

"Which means that if we return to our proper time he will have control over your life," she said.

He surprised her by giving a shake of his head. "No one controls my life."

"But—" She hesitated. This male was unpredictably sensitive about his half-breed status. "Isn't he your master?"

"Not anymore," he said. "Baine offered me my freedom nearly a century ago."

She felt a stab of surprise. It was rare for a master to release a servant. They had a belief that every creature should be delighted to be their slaves for an eternity.

"Why do you stay?" she demanded.

A smile curved Char's lips, easing his grim expression. There was no mistaking his affection for Baine.

"Because he's my friend."

Her heart gave a funny jerk. As if someone had attached a string to it and was giving it a tug.

"Loyalty," she breathed.

She moved closer to his side, but before she could continue, a pulse of heat slammed into her back.

Dragon.

Her muscles tensed as she turned to watch the male step into the corridor behind them.

He was a pureblood with a short, stocky form that was covered by a formal golden robe trimmed with rubies the size of her fists. He had long, dark hair and dark eyes, with deeply bronzed skin. She supposed he was handsome, in a rugged sort of way. And he had enough power to make the floor tremble. But she didn't feel any of the zips and zings that ricocheted through her stomach when she glanced at Char.

Instead, her only thought was convincing him to go away without attracting attention.

"Do not move," the stranger commanded.

His arrogant tone, not to mention the over-the-top robe, revealed that he was a guest of her father, not a guard. Still, he clearly expected her to obey his order.

Blayze angled her chin so her nose was in the air. It was a trick her mother used when she wanted to intimidate someone.

"Is something wrong?" she demanded.

The male frowned, moving toward them. "This is the private quarters of the lair."

Char instinctively angled his body until he was half standing in front of her, his aggression filling the air with a searing heat. "I am aware of our location," he said.

The dragon's nose flared, a curl of smoke trailing from his nostril.

"I was speaking to your mistress," he reprimanded Char.

Flames danced over Char's skin, and Blayze was swift to move so she was the one standing in front of him. What was wrong with the foolish male? He was going to get himself killed.

"Did Synge send you to follow me?" she asked the dragon.

There was a tense pause before the dragon moved his gaze from Char back to Blayze.

"He mentioned that you were worried that there was a plot to harm his unborn child," he admitted.

Blayze was confused. If Synge wanted to keep an eye on them, why not send a guard?

"Are you a member of his clan?" she asked.

The dragon arched a brow, as if amazed that Blayze didn't instantly recognize him.

Typical dragon conceit.

"I am Bolt, son of Ash, and I am certain you have heard that I am to be betrothed to Synge's daughter."

Char's breath hissed through his teeth. This time, however, he managed to keep his lips closed.

A miracle.

Blayze concentrated on the dragon in front of her.

"You are Bolt?" she asked, finding it impossible to visualize this male as her mate.

Yes, she'd already determined he was handsome. And powerful. And wearing jewels that revealed he had an impressive hoard.

All the things most females desired in a male.

But the mere thought of being bonded to a male who wasn't Char made her shudder in horror.

Unaware of her dark thoughts, Bolt gave a small dip of his head. "Yes. And you?"

"Blayze, from the clan of Ravel," Blayze said, offering a formal curtsy.

It was awkward, but it was good enough to fool the male who was clearly more concerned with her presence in this particular corridor.

"You have not answered why you are in the private quarters," he reminded her, allowing his power to hum in the air.

A less than subtle warning.

And one Char couldn't ignore.

He shouldered his way to her side, glaring at the other male. "Because we don't have to."

Bolt stepped forward, releasing even more of his power. The torches rattled and dust fell from the ceiling.

Crap. This encounter was going downhill fast.

She had to do something before the males decided to do more than glare and blow smoke at each other.

"Char." She laid her hand on his arm, careful to move slowly. An angry dragon, even a half-breed one, could do all sorts of bad things if he was startled. "Perhaps it would be best if I speak with Bolt alone."

He turned his head, his eyes a molten silver as he glared at her in disbelief. "No way in hell."

Bolt moved until he was just a foot away, his beefy hands clenched into fists. "You will not speak to your mistress in that manner."

Char's skin began to shimmer as his inner beast demanded release. Any other time Blayze would have been amazed. It was rare for a half-breed to be capable of shifting.

Plus, he had the magic of his fey mother.

A dangerous combination.

Still, he didn't have the power to take on a pureblood dragon.

"You—"

"Char." She turned so she was standing directly in front of him, her fingers pressing against his lips. "We can't risk attracting attention."

Char reluctantly transferred his gaze from Bolt to her pleading expression. His eyes continued to smolder with silver fire.

"That is precisely what I said before you insisted on heading into the throne room," he growled.

"Why do you allow your servant to display such disrespect?" Bolt demanded, blatantly trying to provoke Char into a fight.

Blayze rolled her eyes. She didn't have much experience with males, but she was already discovering they were aggravating creatures.

"Char," she said in soft, soothing tones. "Trust me."

He didn't want to. It was obvious in his tightly clenched expression and the sparks that continued to hover in the air around him. But with an obvious effort, he forced himself to take a deep breath. And then another.

At last he managed to overcome his primal male urge to shield her from any danger.

"I'll give you five minutes," he rasped, glancing toward Bolt. "Touch her and I'll kill you."

Bolt's eyes narrowed, but Blayze gave Char a small shove before the two could start exchanging blows. Or worse, dragon-fire.

"Go," she pleaded.

He did. But not without a lot of glowering and stomping his feet. Blayze swallowed a sigh, waiting until he was around the curve of the corridor before she turned to meet Bolt's burning gaze.

"That servant is in dire need of discipline," he informed her.

She smiled wryly. "Yes, I know."

A portion of the seething anger eased as Bolt focused his attention fully on her. That didn't make him any less dangerous. But at least he wasn't considering the pleasure of following Char and ripping him into tiny shreds.

"Who are you?" he demanded.

Blayze wrinkled her nose. She didn't remind him that she'd already given him her name and clan. That wasn't what he was asking.

He wanted to know if she was there to hurt Synge or his unborn child. And he wasn't going be satisfied with some vague story.

Which meant she either came up with a convincing lie or she told him the truth.

Really, there was no choice.

She'd been mentally connected to her mother. Which meant she'd never developed the talent for deceiving others.

She sucked in a deep breath. She was about to put her life in the hands of this stranger, and she had no idea if he was going to help her or kill her on the spot.

A realization that would make any dragon's heart beat a little faster.

"This is going to be difficult to believe," she warned him.

Bolt waved an impatient hand. "Explain."

"I am your betrothed."

Silence. The sort of silence that was tangible. Like a heavy weight sitting on her chest. She was smart enough not to break it.

"Are you jesting?" he at last demanded.

"No." She gave a somber shake of her head. "Indeed, nothing has ever been so serious. At least for me."

His brows snapped together. "My betrothed has not been born."

She waved a hand toward the wooden bench that was set beneath a brightly burning torch. It didn't look particularly comfortable, but it would have to do.

"Perhaps we could have a seat?" she suggested.

Bolt glanced around. Probably searching to see if this was a trap. Then he offered a grudging nod of his head. "Very well."

Together they perched on the narrow bench, and, clearing her throat, Blayze offered a condensed version of her life. She told him about the curse when she'd been just a baby. She told him about the Council condemning her to death and her mother's frantic effort to keep her hidden while protecting her from the evil magic. She told him about Char's magic that had given her a temporary reprieve, and her own ability to use the curse to pull herself backward through the centuries until she'd arrived in this time and place.

He listened in silence, his expression unreadable. Then, as she stopped speaking to give him the opportunity to absorb her wild tale, he released a harsh breath.

"So you are Synge's daughter," he said. He spoke the words slowly.

Was he was trying to make sure that he'd heard her right? Or maybe just trying to determine if she was utterly delusional.

"I know it sounds crazy, but yes, I'm Synge's daughter," she assured him.

He reached to grasp her chin, gently tilting her face upward so he could study her with a searching gaze.

"I can sense his blood," he abruptly said. "And your eyes are the same as your mother's."

She offered a tentative smile. "I'm sorry. I know this must be confusing."

Surprisingly, he gave a small shrug. "It is an astonishing tale, but I have encountered another dragon who possessed the rare talent of manipulating magic," he told her. "I believe you."

Blayze felt a stab of relief. She hadn't expected him to be so easily convinced that she was speaking the truth. Honestly, she'd half expected Bolt to be calling for the guards so she could be hauled to the dungeons.

Or simply blasted with his fire.

It took a minute for her to realize that he was still studying her. Like she was a weird, not entirely pleasant puzzle.

"You are looking at me strangely," she said.

"You are my mate." His expression remained stoic, but there was something that might have been pain smoldering in the back of his dark eyes. Was his dragon wounded? "You have gone from a distant future to a flesh and blood reality."

"That troubles you?" she demanded.

"I am…" His hand dropped as he sought the proper words to explain his feelings. "Pleased," he at last said. "You are even more beautiful than I could ever have dreamed. And you have courage that would make any mate proud."

She tilted her head to the side. She didn't miss the hollowness in his tone. Another female might take offense at his obvious lack of pleasure in meeting his betrothed. But Blayze had never had the opportunity to develop the same sense of vanity as other females. Instead, she found herself sympathizing with the male's inner pain.

"Very pretty, but I can sense your heart belongs to another," she said.

Bolt turned his head, casting a glance down the corridor. Was he nervous?

That was odd.

Few things could make a full-grown dragon jumpy.

"Who told you that?"

"Your eyes," she admitted.

He grimaced before he was arranging his features back into a smooth mask. "It is not meant to be."

"Why not?"

"My father has decided that it is my duty to align our clan with Synge."

She wrinkled her nose. "Just as my father decided it was the duty of his unborn daughter to give him the power necessary to challenge for a seat on the Council."

His eyes widened, as if he was startled by the fact she knew Synge was angling to gain the ultimate power. Clearly he did not realize that particular piece of gossip was running rampant through the gathered guests.

Then, he gave a small nod. "Precisely."

She squared her shoulders. Bolt didn't want this mating. Which meant she might be able to convince him to help her. At the very least, she could convince him not to stand in her path.

"I am here to alter our futures," she promised in a soft voice.

"Alter the future?" He frowned in confusion. "What does that mean?"

She paused. She had enough knowledge of males to realize that Bolt would dig in his feet if he thought she was asking him to betray his loyalty to his clan.

"Perhaps we can both seek happiness rather than duty," she finally said.

As expected, he gave a sharp shake of his head. "My father will never allow me to break the betrothal."

"Never say never," she warned him. "I believe in miracles."

Without warning, he glanced down corridor. "Does your miracle include your servant?"

Warmth raced through her blood at the thought of Char. Even out of sight she could feel him. She sensed his frustration and fear at being forced to stay away. And his pounding need to know that she was safe.

Barely realizing what she was doing, she reached out with her mind to offer him comfort. Instantly he reached back, offering a mental stroke that sent a tingle of pleasure snaking down her spine.

A small smile curved her lips.

So that was that.

There was no way she could have so easily connected to Char if he wasn't her true mate.

"Yes, I suppose he is a miracle," she agreed.

Blayze felt a hot color stain her cheeks, but thankfully, Bolt didn't ask for more information. He obviously sensed that she was closer to a mere half-breed than she should be. But since she hadn't interrogated him when it came to the female he preferred, he offered her the same respect for her privacy.

"You said that you used the curse to travel back to this time?"

Happy to return the conversation to more pressing matters, she swiveled on the bench to face him. She wanted him to see her expression and know that she was determined to succeed in her goals.

"Yes. I thought it would bring me to the precise time that the curse was cast, but instead it seems to have brought me to the time that the curse was smuggled into this lair."

He gave a slow nod. "So you'll discover who is responsible?"

"Char already managed to discover who was responsible."

"Who?"

"A dragon named Magma."

"Bastard." With a low roar, Bolt was on his feet, bluish flames swirling around his body. "I am not surprised that he would be the traitor."

Blayze rose from the bench, inwardly pleased by Bolt's reaction. "Why aren't you surprised?"

"It has been whispered for many years that he is a dragon without honor," Bolt said. "Not only has he broken contracts, and stolen from his own clansmen, but he has used nefarious means to defeat his enemies rather than facing them in open battle."

Blayze felt a surge of anger as she thought of the dragon who was evil enough to use black magic on a mere hatchling to keep his position of power.

"He is obviously willing to go to any lengths to maintain his place with the Council."

Bolt continued to look disgusted, but it was the hint of resolve hardening his features that gave her a tiny burst of hope.

"The male will pay for his treachery," he growled.

She lifted a warning hand. "First I must track down the servant who has the curse."

He frowned. "Magma used one of his servants to bring the curse to the lair?"

She shook her head. "Not one of his," she corrected. "One of my father's."

He stiffened in shock. "You are certain?"

"Yes."

Bolt clenched his hands, his flames continuing to dance over his body. "We should warn Synge."

"We've already tried to tell him that there is danger," she told him. "My father refuses to believe that anyone would dare and try to attack him in his own lair. And if Magma learns we have discovered his plan he will either strike out and cause a war between clans, or he will find another way to hurt my father." She held his dark gaze. "Or even you."

Bolt was immediately offended by her warning. He bristled with male pride, puffing out his chest. "He does not frighten me."

Blayze rolled her eyes. "Are all males the same?" she demanded.

He pretended he didn't hear her. "How do you intend to learn which servant has the curse?"

"My hope is that I can sense the magic," she said, grimacing as she realized it didn't sound like a very good plan when she said it out loud.

Bolt, however, merely nodded. "And when you find him?"

She blinked. Why did people continue to ask such a stupid question?

"I'll kill him, of course."

CHAPTER TWELVE

Levet paced from one end of the tiled floor to the other. Back and forth. Back and forth. His tail swished behind him and his wings were drooping.

It'd been over an hour since they'd entered Blayze's private chamber. Vex continued to perch on the edge of the bed, her eyes closed while Tayla watched her with a growing impatience.

"What's she doing?" Tayla at last burst out.

Levet halted his pacing to glance toward Vex. The succubus didn't move, but he could feel the hum of her power. It didn't have the erotic edge that most succubi used, but it still sent tiny tingles of pleasure through his body.

"She is searching for Blayze's mental imprint," he said, his gaze swiveling toward Tayla.

The imp folded her arms around her waist. Her pretty face was pale and tight with strain. Levet swallowed a sigh. He hated to see her so stressed-up. No wait…stressed out.

"Why is it taking so long?" Tayla demanded.

Vex abruptly lifted her lashes, her golden eyes dark with frustration.

"Because the dragon is either dead or in another dimension," she announced in clipped tones.

"Dead?" Tayla gasped, pressing a hand to the center of her chest. "No. I refuse to believe that fate could be so cruel."

Vex shrugged. Unlike Tayla and Levet, the succubus had nothing to lose if someone had managed to kill Blayze.

"Haven't you heard? Fate is a bitch," Vex retorted. Then she gave another shrug. "But I do feel a distant echo which makes me believe that she might still be alive. It's almost as if she has traveled…"

Vex allowed her words to trail away.

"Where?" Tayla prompted, eager to latch on to any thread of hope.

Vex released a harsh sigh. "I am not sure."

Levet waddled forward, laying a small hand on Vex's knee. "Can you try to reach her?" he asked.

Vex paused, glancing toward Tayla before returning her gaze to Levet. "I will try, but I can't make any promises," she said.

"Merci, ma belle." Levet patted her knee, a strained smile curving his lips. "And just as a teensy, tiny reminder, my future health depends solely on you locating Blayze."

Vex scowled, clearly feeling the pressure. "Then maybe you should leave me alone to do my business," she snapped.

"Oui." Levet wisely stepped away. See? He had no death wish. "Do your business."

Vex glared at him before closing her eyes. Levet

continued to back away, joining Tayla who had moved to stand in the open doorway. Far enough away to give the succubus space, but still capable of keeping an eye on her.

"What happens if she does find Blayze's mental imprint?" Tayla asked in a soft voice, as if worried she might draw the wrath of Vex if she spoke too loud.

She should be worried.

Vex was called Vex for a reason. She was beautiful and passionate and glorious fun. But she had the temper of a rabid goblin.

"Then she can latch on to her and use the connection to physically yank her back to this room."

Tayla looked suitably impressed. It was one thing to be able to mentally communicate with another demon. Levet possessed that particular skill. But to actually be able to mentally grab on tight enough to transport them from one spot to another was amazing.

"Does she pull them through a portal?" Tayla asked.

Levet gave a lift of his hands. "I've never seen her actually do it."

Tayla sighed, chewing on her lower lip. "I hope this works."

Levet's tail twitched. Styx's warning was still ringing in his ears. "As do I."

* * *

Styx left The Viper Pit's rooftop, where a shimmering dome of magic held the ancient dragon in stasis.

The magical spell thankfully continued to keep Synge imprisoned in a deep sleep, but Styx remained on edge. With every passing second they came closer to Synge breaking free of the spell and starting a war that none of them wanted.

And the worst part was that there wasn't a damned thing he could do about it.

He had no way of discovering which vampire might have released the curse. Not when it had happened over five hundred years ago. Which meant he had to depend on Levet to track down Blayze and return her to her father's lair.

Was it any wonder his stomach felt it was being tied into a tight knot of dread?

No demon with a brain in his skull would want to place the fate of the world in the hands of that damned gargoyle.

Returning to the balcony of the club, he found Viper waiting for him.

"Where's Baine?" the younger vampire demanded.

"I asked him to remain and keep an eye on his father," Styx said. "I'd like a little warning if the stasis spell starts to fail."

Viper grimaced. "I'd like more than just a 'little' warning," he muttered.

No shit. The knot in Styx's gut doubled in size.

He moved to glance over the railing. The long room was empty, but he could sense fey creatures still scurrying below him.

"I thought you were going to empty the place of guests?"

Viper gave an elegant wave of his hand. The younger vampire would forever be a Regency aristocrat at heart.

"There are a few pixies hiding in the cellars. They managed to lock themselves in one of the storage closets and refuse to come out."

Styx snorted. Fey looked fragile, but they were cunning beasts who would take advantage of any situation. "They probably took a few bottles of your brandy with them," he pointed out.

Viper arched a brow. "Speaking of my precious brandy, I do hope you intend to make sure the enraged dragon who is perched on my roof doesn't destroy my club."

Styx instinctively glanced toward the ceiling. It didn't matter that he couldn't see Synge. He could feel his presence pressing down on them with a heavy sense of doom.

"I'm more concerned about the enraged dragon destroying me," he admitted.

Viper tugged at the lacy cuff of his shirt that peeked from the sleeve of his velvet coat.

"Well that would be a shame, of course," he drawled. "But not as tragic as the loss of The Viper Pit."

Styx rolled his eyes. "Your loyalty to your Anasso is touching."

"There can be another Anasso," Viper assured him. "There's only one Viper Pit."

Styx's lips twitched. Being the King of the Vampires was a sucky job that had few rewards. Unfortunately, someone had to do it, and for now the responsibility was squarely on him. "We should be safe for another few hours," he said, inwardly sending a prayer to whatever deity might be listening. In truth, he didn't know how long they had.

"And then?" Viper demanded.

"Then we run," he retorted.

Viper made a sound that revealed what he thought about Styx's plan. At least he didn't flip him off.

"Wouldn't it be easier if you took your big-ass sword to the roof and killed our unwelcome visitor?" the younger vampire asked.

The thought had crossed Styx's mind. More than once.

"I'm trying to avoid a war with the dragons," he

told his companion. "Something that will be easier if I don't kill one of their most powerful leaders. Plus, Baine is up there keeping a watch on his father. He might have something to say about me waving around a pointy weapon."

Viper rolled his eyes. "Buzzkill."

Styx folded his arms over his chest. "As much as I hate to admit it, I have to hope that Levet can find Blayze before all hell breaks loose."

Viper looked grim. "Literally."

CHAPTER THIRTEEN

Char finished his sweep of the empty guardroom. It looked the same as it did five hundred years in the future. No big surprise. Most warriors had zero interest in interior design.

They wanted someplace to practice their skills, store their weapons, and sleep without concern they were going to be attacked.

Simple.

Once he was certain it would be the perfect way to locate the treacherous servant, he stepped into the corridor, and headed back toward Blayze.

He didn't know if it'd been five minutes. And he didn't care.

He could tell himself a thousand times that Blayze could never be his. And that he would have to walk away when she chose a pureblooded mate. Someone like Bolt. But his dragon was restlessly pressing against his skin, refusing to accept the inevitable.

His beast was convinced the female belonged to him. And no amount of logic was going to change his mind.

Rounding the curve of the corridor, he discovered Blayze standing close to Bolt. Instantly his silver flames were dancing over his skin.

"Your time's up," he growled, his gaze locked on Bolt as he continued to move forward.

Blayze made a sound that might have been frustration as she hurried toward him and laid a hand on the center of his chest.

"Bolt has agreed to help us," she said.

The mere sound of the male's name on her lips was enough to make Char's dragon roar in protest.

"We don't need his help," Char snapped.

Blayze frowned. "Of course we do."

"I—" Char snapped his lips together. He was being an idiot. Who would turn away the assistance of a pureblooded dragon? Only a jealous, petty fool, that's who. "Fine," he forced himself to mutter, pivoting on his heel to lead them back down the corridor. Baine had taught him the benefits of using his brain rather than his brawn. Right now, he needed to concentrate on what he'd learned from those lessons. It was the best way to protect Blayze. "Follow me."

Blayze quickened her step to walk at his side, the pulsing heat of Bolt slamming into Char's back as the odd trio moved in silence through the torchlit hall.

They followed the curve of the corridor, before Char led them through an arched opening.

"Where are we going?" Blayze asked in confusion.

They traveled across the open space that was used for training. Bare floor. Bare ceiling. Weapons lining the walls.

"This is the area used by Synge's warriors," Char

explained.

Blayze continued to look confused. "You think the servant is a guard?"

Char shook his head. "No, but there is a connecting door into the servants' quarters."

She tilted her head to the side, regarding him with a questioning glance. "Why go in the back way?"

"The servants aren't used to having guests strolling around in this area," Char pointed out. "It might alert the traitor that something is wrong."

"He makes a sound point," Bolt said. "Our presence will attract unwanted attention."

Char pressed his lips together. He wanted to tell Bolt that he didn't need his damned approval. Unfortunately, he'd already used up his quota for acting like a peevish hatchling. Time to be a big boy and concentrate on destroying the bastard who held the curse.

Blayze glanced around the empty space as they moved from the training area to the sleeping area. "Where are the guards?"

"They're all on duty in other parts of the lair," he said. "Synge is more concerned with the guests in the throne room than what's happening with the servants."

She gave a slow nod. "Okay. I guess that makes sense."

They moved past the barrack-styled cots and out a narrow back entrance. There was a hallway that led to the bathing area in one direction, and in the opposite direction was the entrance to the servants' main quarters.

Char slowed as the air became spiced with the thickening scent of fey and several lesser demons who served Synge.

"How close do you need to be?" he asked in a low voice.

Blayze gave a lift of her hands. "I don't know. I've

never used my magic like this before."

Char grimaced. The last thing he wanted was for Blayze to be near the servant responsible for destroying her life, but he didn't know how else for her to sense the curse. "Through here."

He led them into the dark alcove that offered a view of the large courtyard. It wasn't as stark as the guards' room, but it was still plain, with a few benches, and a table in the center of the floor.

Fewer than a handful of servants were in the courtyard. Some eating a late dinner, and others strolling around the open space before returning to their duties.

Beyond the courtyard was an arched opening that led to the sleeping quarters, but Char was hoping they could remain hidden in the shadows.

"Well?" he asked softly.

Blayze closed her eyes, her hands clutched at her side. Then she sucked in a startled breath. "The curse is here."

His heart jumped with a fierce surge of hope. Whether they got back to their time or not, the first priority was ensuring that they got rid of the curse.

"You're sure?" he asked.

"Yes."

"Can you tell who has it?"

She took a minute, her gaze skimming over the handful of servants. At last she pointed at a slender male wearing Synge's dark green uniform.

"There. The vampire."

Char studied the male. He was average height with brown hair smoothed into a tail at his nape. His features were pale, and carved into stern lines. Char didn't recognize him.

Which meant he wasn't a servant of Synge's when Char had been in the lair.

Bolt moved to stand at Blayze's side. Char clenched

his teeth. *No punching the dragon*, he silently reminded himself.

"Flynn?" Bolt demanded.

Char glanced toward the dragon. "You know him?"

Bolt arched a brow—a silent reminder that he was a pureblood and above rubbing elbows with the riffraff.

"I know that he is one of the servants Synge uses to collect his tithes from the orcs," he said.

Char glanced back at Flynn. The male possessed the arrogant expression of all vampires, but it was the sneer on his thin lips and the way that he held himself aloof from the others that revealed he thought he was far too good to be a servant.

"Not a high position," Char murmured. Many demons petitioned dragons for favors, and in return they were asked to pay a tithe. They rarely realized that they would be paying for the rest of eternity. Those servants most favored were sent to collect the tithes from the fey or harpies. The least favored were stuck with orcs and trolls. "Perhaps Magma promised a more prestigious place in his lair."

"Possible," Bolt agreed.

Blayze ignored both of them. Her attention was focused like a laser on the vampire.

"I'm going to kill him," she rasped, taking a step forward.

Char reached out to grasp her upper arm, bringing her to a sharp halt. "Hold on, Xena, Warrior Princess. You can't just charge in there," he warned.

She turned her head to glare at him. "Why not?"

He brushed his hand lightly over her cheek, hoping his touch would help to ease her fury. He sympathized with her urge to destroy the vampire. He was feeling his own share of bloodlust.

But they needed to think clearly.

They were too close to risk failure now.

"If he has the vessel containing the curse on him, he'll cast it to protect himself," he said, as much to remind himself not to do something stupid as to keep her at his side. "Which means all of this will be for nothing."

She scowled. "Then what do you suggest?"

He'd already considered the best way to approach the servant if they managed to track him down.

"I'll go in and lure him out," he said. "No one will question my presence."

Her scowl remained. "How will you lure him?"

Without warning, Bolt stepped forward. "I will do it."

Char sent him a frustrated glare. Was the male trying to play the hero in front of Blayze? Or was he one of those dragons who always had to be in charge?

"We just established that a pureblood would cause too much chaos," Char reminded him, an edge in his voice.

Bolt tilted back his head so he could peer down the length of his nose. "I am soon to become a member of Synge's clan," he drawled. "Flynn would have no choice but to agree to follow me if I said that Synge had need of him in the throne room."

Char hissed at the reminder that Bolt was about to become formally betrothed to Blayze. Then, with a valiant effort, he forced himself to ignore the deliberate provocation.

He couldn't afford distractions until the vampire was dead.

After that he would worry about how he was going to deal with his dragon's determination to claim Blayze as his own.

He offered a stiff nod of his head. Bolt was right. The vampire would have no choice but to follow him if Bolt told him that Synge had need of his services.

"Give us time to set up an ambush," he

commanded.

Bolt waved a dismissive hand. "I do not need your assistance to kill a vampire."

Char's lips parted, but before he could speak, Blayze was moving to stand directly in front of the dragon.

"Bolt, he is holding a powerful curse that destroyed my family," she softly murmured, laying her hand on his arm. "You would have no protection if he cast it in your direction. We must catch him off guard."

Bolt's jaw jutted forward, but he had no defense against Blayze's pleading gaze. He finally conceded defeat. "If you insist."

"I do," she said.

Char moved, placing a possessive arm around her shoulders. At the same time, he tugged her away from the dragon. He was trying to remain focused on the danger, but there was no need for any touching between the two dragons.

"Give us time to find the best place for an attack," he warned.

Bolt glanced toward Blayze before offering a grudging nod.

Char clenched his teeth and urged her to head back out the way they came. Acting like an adult was proving to be harder than he expected.

Almost as if determined to rub salt in his open wounds, Blayze glanced over her shoulder. "I hope he doesn't do anything stupid," she whispered.

Char felt his stomach clench, his dragon sulking at her concerned expression. "You're worried about him."

Obviously sensing his annoyance, she sent him a chiding glance. "I certainly don't want anything bad to happen to him."

"I see."

She heaved a small sigh. "Char—"

"We need to hurry," he interrupted, pausing to make sure there was no one in the corridor before they stepped out of the guardroom.

They moved at a quick pace, a growing sense of urgency tingling through Char.

"Bolt has no more interest in being my mate than I have in being his," she abruptly said, easily keeping up with his long strides.

He tried to concentrate on his surroundings. Just because the vampire was behind them, that didn't mean there wasn't some potential danger lurking just ahead.

In fact, it was almost guaranteed.

But there was no way he could resist a quick glance at Blayze's delicate profile.

There was only so much adulting a poor half-dragon could do.

"He told you that?"

"He didn't have to," she assured him. "I could sense he's already given his heart to another."

His gaze snapped back to the shadows ahead of them, his lips thinning.

"Dragons don't follow their hearts when it comes to their mate," he reminded her.

Her fingers brushed down his back. "Some of us do."

Oh, hell. His insides felt all gooey. As if she'd melted him with her dragon-fire.

The sensation should have been embarrassing. He was a sophisticated male who'd been a favorite among females for centuries, not a silly hatchling. Instead, he savored the warmth spreading through his body.

At least he was trying to savor it until an oppressive power began to spread through the air.

Instantly he was on full alert.

"Dragon," he breathed, coming to an abrupt halt. He easily recognized the scent. "Magma."

Blayze stood next to him, her eyes wide. "What's he doing here?"

That was the million-dollar question.

Char recalled the conversation he'd overheard. Magma had been a leader who clearly depended on brute strength and treachery to remain in power. Which meant he would assume everyone was like him.

Untrustworthy and plotting to double-cross him.

"Perhaps he wants to make certain that Flynn understands the danger of not following through on his commitment to betray Synge," he suggested. "Or maybe he saw Bolt following us from the throne room and became suspicious."

Blayze squared her shoulders. "I have to get rid of him before he can warn the vampire."

Once again Char was forced to reach out and grasp her arm before she could charge into a fight. "You are certainly Synge's daughter."

She sent him a wary frown. "What does that mean?"

He hesitated. Probably best not to share his opinion that she had a habit of choosing violence to solve every situation.

Instead, he grasped her shoulders and stared down at her upturned face. He didn't have to be a prophet to know that things were going to escalate quickly unless they managed to distract the approaching dragon.

"You need to prepare the ambush," he told her.

She studied his face. Clearly she sensed he was hiding something from her.

"What are you going to do?" she demanded.

There was no time to think of a convincing lie. Already the air was sweltering with Magma's power as he came closer and closer. Within a few seconds it would be too late for Blayze to escape unnoticed.

"I'm going to get rid of the dragon," he said, giving

her a firm push backward, straight through the doorway.

Her eyes widened. "Char, no."

"Trust me," he commanded, reaching out to grab the door and firmly close it. Then, with a twist of his hand, he crushed the knob until it was hopelessly jammed.

It wouldn't hold her for long, but he only needed a couple of minutes to lure Magma away.

Hurrying down the corridor, he didn't worry about the fact he was just about to confront a pureblood dragon who'd already proven he was willing to sink into the gutters to win. All that mattered was keeping Blayze safe.

Period. End of story.

He'd nearly returned to the public area of the lair when he rounded a corner to discover the large dragon with long black hair standing in the center of the corridor.

Magma.

The dragon was still wearing his gaudy crimson robe, and his expression remained arrogant, but Char caught a whiff of fear coming from the male. As if Magma was worrying about the success of his daring plan.

He should be worried.

Once Synge realized he'd been betrayed, he was going to go apeshit.

And when a pureblood dragon went apeshit, bad things happened. Earthquakes. Molten fire. End of the world.

Realizing that Char had stopped instead of scurrying away like a proper servant, the dragon sent him a warning frown. "Go about your business," he snapped.

Char pressed his hands together, offering a small bow. "You are Magma?"

The dragon glowered with impatience. "I am."

"Then this is a most fortunate meeting," he murmured in the smarmy tones a servant was expected to use. "A vampire by the name of Flynn requested that I seek you out."

Magma froze, abruptly centering his attention fully on Char. "Why?"

"He needs to meet with you," Char told him.

Magma's glower remained intact. "Where is he?"

"This way." Char waved a hand toward a nearby fork in the corridor.

"Why did he send you?" Magma demanded, warily following Char as he headed into the side tunnel that led toward the less populated area of the lair. "If he wishes to speak with me he could have come himself."

Char quickened his pace. Magma wouldn't be fooled for long. The farther away from Blayze he could get, the better.

"He mentioned that he was in fear that your gift for Synge is in danger," he told the dragon, sweat dripping down his spine. Even as a half-dragon he reacted to the heat that Magma was pumping into the air. Was it on purpose? Or just a symptom of the stress the dragon was under? "He is trying to protect it."

"And who are you?"

"I owe Flynn a debt," Char said, his gaze searching for a suitable spot to try and corner the dangerous beast. At least long enough for Blayze and Bolt to kill Flynn. After that…well, one problem at a time. He spotted an opening into what looked like an old torture chamber. Perfect. "One that is now paid," he told the dragon, stepping aside to point into the dark room. "He's in here."

Magma tilted back his head, sniffing the air. "Why do I not sense him?"

"He is attempting to disguise his presence," Char

assured the large male.

Magma's nose flared, his eyes smoldering with a crimson fire. "Liar," he growled. "This is a trap."

A shimmer of power swirled around Magma's large body. A warning he was about to shift.

Char didn't hesitate.

There was no way in hell he could battle Magma once he was in his dragon-form. Not if he hoped to live through the encounter.

His hand started to reach for the diamond-knife tucked at his lower back, only to realize that he wasn't going to have time to do the necessary damage.

So instead, he used the only advantage he possessed.

Lifting his hand, he released the fey magic that bubbled through his blood. Instantly a spiderweb of sparkling strands floated through the air.

Magma was still in the process of shifting when the threads of magic wrapped around him, slowing time and freezing him in place.

It was a temporary solution.

Char had expended a lot of energy over the past hours and he could already feel the strain of maintaining his spell. His only hope was that he could hold on long enough for Blayze to destroy the curse.

CHAPTER FOURTEEN

Blayze turned to discover that she was in the same room they'd arrived in. The room that would eventually become her nursery.

Her first instinct was to break down the door and rush to protect Char. For all of his courage, he was no match for a pureblood dragon.

But his last words continued to echo in her mind.

Trust me.

How often had she demanded that he offer her his trust? To insist that he believe in her ability to make her own decisions?

Now that the shoe was on the other foot, she discovered it wasn't as easy as she assumed. In fact, it was taking every ounce of her willpower to accept that

Char could handle the large dragon.

Closing her eyes, she sucked in a deep breath and tried to clear her mind. Any second, Bolt would be coming down the corridor with the vampire. She couldn't afford to be distracted.

Almost as if to mock her grim determination to be prepared, there was a sudden tingle of power that crawled across her back. With a muffled gasp, she spun on her heel, her gaze searching the shadows that filled the room.

Nothing.

With a frown, she took a tentative step forward.

"Hello. Who's there?" she called out softly. There was another prickle of power. There was definitely magic in the air. But where was it coming from? "Hello?"

She moved to press her hand against the wall. It was warm. Not that unusual in a dragon lair. But she sensed that this was different. And there was the scent of…stone?

Gargoyle?

That seemed unlikely. From what she could determine from her mother, dragons and gargoyles were natural enemies.

Of course, most demons were enemies to dragons.

Still trying to process what the strange tingles could mean, she was jerked back to attention as the smell of stone was abruptly replaced with the scorching power of Bolt along with the dry, raspy scent of a vampire.

They were coming.

Shaking off her unease, Blayze focused on her inner beast. Usually she was in a maddened state from her curse when she shifted. This time she allowed it happen in a slow, carefully controlled burst of power.

Heat and ecstasy flowed through her, an intoxicating brew of magic that made her feel giddy with pleasure. She shuddered, her body stretching and popping as her wings spread to a ten-foot span and her narrow head bumped into the ceiling.

At the same time her senses heightened to a near painful awareness.

She could feel the heavy stone of the lair that surrounded her. And the distant buzz of dragons in the throne room. More importantly, she could sense the precise moment that the vampire realized he was being led into an ambush.

It was in the spiked scent of adrenaline and the low curse that Flynn muttered just before Blayze smashed through the wall and surged forward.

Unfortunately, Blayze expected Flynn to try and bolt down the corridor. Which meant she'd missed destroying him with her dragon-fire when the vampire instead darted past her with a blinding speed, leaping through the opening she'd created and into the nursery.

***

Levet was counting each tick of the clock. Just a couple of hours to sunrise. And the looming possibility that his head would be mounted on a wall in Styx's lair.

Not the most pleasant thought.

Perhaps he truly should consider an extended vacation in a remote locale.

Like Hades. Or Vegas.

His dark thoughts were suddenly interrupted as Vex surged to her feet.

"I sense her," she announced.

Both Levet and Tayla rushed forward, nearly tripping over their feet in an effort to reach the succubus.

"She's alive?" Tayla demanded.

Vex gave a small nod. "Yes."

Levet breathed a sigh of relief even as Tayla

pressed her hands to her heart.

"Where is she?" the imp asked.

Vex grimaced. "Not where. When."

Levet's wings twitched. Was she speaking in some sort of strange code?

"I do not understand," he admitted.

Vex gave a lift of her hands, as if uncertain how to explain. "I don't know how, but she's traveled back in time."

Levet's eyes widened. "That is—" He swallowed the word "impossible." Over the past few years he'd discovered that there was very little that wasn't possible. "Can you contact her?" he asked instead.

She shoved her fingers through the short strands of her hair, suddenly appearing unbearably tired. "I'm going to try."

Levet reached out to lightly touch her hand. "What can we do to help?"

"Make sure I'm not interrupted," Vex said, once again perching on the edge of the bed.

Together Levet and Tayla returned to their position beside the door. Neither wanted to interfere with Vex's attempt to latch on to Blayze.

Her success was too important to risk.

Levet pressed his back against the jamb while Tayla twisted her hands together in a nervous gesture.

"It must have been Char," she abruptly said, her words so low that Levet could barely catch them.

Levet sent her a startled glance. He'd thought that Tayla was fond of Baine's most trusted servant. "Why do you say that?"

She looked troubled, her face ashen from the strain of the past few hours. "He's the only one who can manipulate time."

Levet considered her words. He had no love for the dragons. Indeed, he found them almost as annoying as the vampires. An amazing feat.

But he couldn't believe that Char would betray Baine.

Besides, the half-breed didn't have the skills necessary to whisk Blayze away.

"*Non*, he can only slow time," he reminded his companion. "He could not physically transport himself into the past."

A portion of Tayla's tension eased, although her expression remained worried. Until Blayze was returned, the looming war between dragons and vampires remained a very real possibility.

"Then what other explanation is there?" she asked.

Levet furrowed his brow. He didn't know any demons capable of sneaking into a dragon's lair and then traveling through time. It would have taken an enormous amount of power.

The kind of power only a dragon possessed.

"What is Blayze's magic?"

Tayla blinked, clearly caught off guard by his question. "I don't know."

Levet gave a lift of his hands, knowing that he was grasping at…hmm…what was it? Hay? Grass?

Straw.

Grasping at straws.

Still, he had no other theory.

"If she has the ability to travel through time, she might have decided to go into the past," he said.

Tayla stiffened, as if she was offended by his words. "Why would she want to leave? She just came home."

Ah. She thought he was implying that Blayze was attempting to flee from her family, including Tayla's mate, Baine.

"It would be the only way to escape her curse," he pointed out in gentle tones.

"Oh." Tayla caught her bottom lip between her teeth, considering Levet's words. "And if we force her to return?"

Levet grimaced. The more he considered his wild theory, the more likely it seemed to be. After all, Blayze was already in the lair, which would answer the question of why Levet had not been able to detect the scent of an intruder.

Of course, he didn't know why she would take Char with her, unless his magic remained tangled with her and it had been an accident.

Oui. That made sense.

Satisfied with the explanation, he turned his thoughts to solving the puzzle of what would happen if Vex could manage to grasp onto the dragon's mind and pull her back through time.

His wings drooped, his stomach suddenly feeling icky. "Then it is quite likely the curse will return."

Tayla gave a soft gasp, but before she could speak, Vex was calling out in satisfaction.

"I think I have her."

"Vex." Levet waddled forward, his tail stuck straight out behind him. "Wait."

CHAPTER FIFTEEN

Blayze roared. Her hulking size was a stupendous benefit when a dragon was soaring through open skies or fighting armies spread across a battlefield.

Not so great in the cramped confines of the lair.

Awkwardly turning toward the room, she watched as the vampire skidded to a halt near the back wall. He was just realizing that he'd managed to trap himself.

With a sizzle of magic, Blayze returned to her human form. She didn't have the same power, but she was far more agile. Something that seemed important as Flynn lifted his hand to reveal a small, ceramic pot.

The curse.

"No, stay back," Flynn warned.

"Blayze, be careful," Bolt said as he stepped through the rubble that had once been the doorway.

The vampire glared at the male dragon. "Why did you deceive me?"

It was Blayze who answered. "Because you intend to betray your master."

The vampire glared at them, his arrogant expression not entirely capable of hiding his fear as his eyes darted from side to side.

He knew he was cornered. Which only made him more dangerous.

"A lie," he hissed, curling back his lips to reveal his massive fangs.

Blayze ignored his pointy teeth. They couldn't hurt her. The only thing she feared was the vessel he had clenched in his hand.

Bolt eased his way along the wall, moving slowly enough he didn't startle the vampire.

"We already know that you are scheming with Magma to destroy Synge," Bolt said.

"A dangerous accusation," the vampire snapped.

"Yes, very dangerous. I can assure you that he will destroy you once he discovers what you have been plotting," Bolt drawled, continuing to circle the room.

Realizing that Bolt was hoping to get close enough to grab the clay pot, Blayze stepped forward, drawing the vampire's attention in her direction.

"Actually, it's much more likely he'll be kept alive so Synge can torture him," she said in musing tones. "He is a dragon who loves to cause pain to those who dare betray him."

The vampire lost a hint of his arrogance, his expression hard as he considered the best way to survive the next few minutes. "What do you want?" he finally asked.

"Why would you betray your master?" Blayze demanded, still trying to keep Flynn focused on her.

The vampire narrowed his gaze, an ugly expression settling on his pale face. "Dragons are not the only demons with ambition."

"You wanted a promotion?" she scoffed.

The vampire looked confused, unfamiliar with the term. "I desired my freedom."

Blayze rolled her eyes. Was the vampire stupid?

"And you believe Magma would have released you from your service?" she asked. "He is a dragon without honor."

Flynn shrugged. "He would have no choice. If I revealed what he had done, he would be destroyed by the other Council members."

Blayze gave a slow shake of her head. The vampire obviously had more ambition than brains. Magma would turn him into a pile of ash the second he'd served his purpose.

But before she could tell Flynn he was an idiot, she was distracted as the strange tingles returned.

What the hell was going on?

She shivered, trying to resist the urge to look over her shoulder. It could be a trick. Perhaps a servant loyal to Magma was lurking nearby just trying to confuse her.

Unfortunately, she must have given some hint that her attention had wavered. Or maybe Flynn belatedly realized that Bolt was getting close enough to rip off his head—one certain way to kill a vampire.

Whichever spooked him, the vampire lifted the clay pot and with one mighty heave was tossing it directly at Blayze.

Three things happened all at once.

Blayze instinctively ducked as the vessel sailed across the room. Bolt leaped forward to place his large body between her and the incoming curse. And a strangely erotic blast of magic filled the air.

Knocked off balance, Blayze tumbled backward, smacking her head against the floor. Bolt, however, stayed standing directly in the path of the curse.

"Bolt, no," she cried out, watching in horror as he

remained in front of her, clearly determined to play the hero.

But even as she tried to scramble upright, the unknown magic gave a violent pulse, and in the blink of an eye, Bolt was gone.

Just like that.

At the same time, the vessel flew over her head and hit the wall behind her. The fragile ceramic smashed on impact, releasing the curse harmlessly into the air.

Shocked silence briefly paralyzed Blayze as she tried to sort through what had just happened. The sight of Flynn tossing the curse. Bolt dashing to stand in front of her.

And then...

Poof. He was gone.

Had Flynn done something? No. That was impossible. Vampires didn't have the ability to create magic.

So had it been a portal? Or did Bolt possess some strange power that allowed him to simply disappear?

Dazed, she slowly rose to her feet, giving a small shake of her head.

She was still struggling to clear her brain when there was a blur of motion. *Damn.* Flynn was trying to escape.

Fury boiled through her. A white-hot, ancient anger that carried the force of a volcano.

This was the evil monster who'd cursed her.

He was going to pay.

With a low growl, she lunged toward his fleeing form, knocking him to the ground before he ever made it out of the room. Then, forgetting the centuries she'd devoted to imagining the various tortures she intended to inflict on the creature responsible for her misery, she allowed her fingers to shift into massive claws.

"Save a place for Magma in the underworld," she

hissed before she was swiping her claws across his throat, easily slicing off his head.

She was turning away from Flynn as a dark burst of energy surrounded his body and it began to disintegrate into a pile of ash.

She no longer had an interest in the vampire who'd destroyed her life. Coming back in time meant that she now had a chance for a future. That was all that mattered.

Oh, and Char. He mattered most of all.

About to head out through the destroyed wall, Blayze felt the strange magic brush against her skin.

She frowned, instinctively reaching out with her powers.

Immediately she realized that it hadn't come from a dragon. Which meant that Bolt wasn't responsible for his own disappearance.

Her heart missed a sudden beat.

If someone else had created the portal, then that meant...

Hope.

CHAPTER SIXTEEN

Char pressed his back against the wall, gritting his teeth as he struggled to remain upright. A task that would be a lot easier if the furious dragon would stop fighting against the spell that was holding him mid-shift.

The effort to maintain his magic was not only taking its toll on his body, but it was also making it impossible for Char to concentrate on what he intended to do next.

He really, really needed a Plan B.

One that didn't include being melted by dragon flames.

"Release me," Magma commanded, his voice oddly distorted by the spell.

The fact he could speak at all, however, meant that Char was barely keeping him restrained.

"A hard pass on that," Char muttered.

The shimmer around the dragon pulsed as he

continued to struggle to get free. "Did you hear me?" The words were less distorted, and louder. They echoed down the corridor.

"I think the entire lair heard you." Sweat trickled down Char's face, his lungs burning. Was it the heat from Magma, or the strain of trying to maintain his spell? It didn't really matter. "Including Synge, who's going to be very interested in why you were in this area of his home," he told the dragon, hoping it would stop the male from fighting against the magic.

It didn't.

Hell, it only increased his efforts.

"I will destroy you," the male growled.

Char clicked his tongue. "Now is that any way to get me to release you?" he mocked.

Magma grunted, the heat in the air making the stone glow red-hot. "Your magic is weakening."

Char had no witty comeback. His magic wasn't just weakening. It was on the verge of complete collapse.

Then, he was suddenly jerking his head to the side as he belatedly realized that the heat wasn't just coming from Magma. There was another dragon nearby.

One who was becoming intimately familiar to him.

"Blayze," he breathed, watching as she hurried around the curve of the corridor. He swept his gaze over her, a sharp relief twisting his heart. She looked pale and disheveled, but she was alive and seemingly unharmed. Then he felt the heavy power of Magma pressing against his magic and his relief transformed to fear. "Dammit. What are you doing here?"

She ignored the dragon who was surrounded by the shimmer of Char's spell. Almost as if she didn't even notice he was there. Instead, she sent Char a tight smile.

"I think I have a way for us to return to our time."

He studied her in confusion. "How?"

She waved a hand, urging him to follow her. "Come

with me."

He frowned, struggling to accept what she was saying. He'd already resigned himself to dying in this corridor. Now she was saying she could take them home?

"What about Flynn?" he demanded, glancing over her shoulder.

She shrugged. "I killed him."

"And the curse?"

"Gone."

A slow smile curled his lips. He didn't know what he loved more about this female. The fact that she could so easily kick ass, or the fact that she didn't even realize how spectacular she was.

"Good girl," he told her.

The dragon next to them wasn't nearly so impressed with her splendid ability to destroy her enemies. His distorted roar rattled through the corridor, making the floor shake and dust filter from the ceiling.

"What do you want to do with him?" he asked his companion.

Her features hardened as she glanced toward Magma. She seemed to consider her options before giving a reluctant shake of her head.

"I can't risk depleting my power," she admitted, genuine regret threaded through her voice. "How much longer will your magic hold him?"

He grimaced. "Not more than a few minutes."

"Long enough," she assured him.

Frustration coiled through Char. He wanted to destroy Magma. He wanted to physically pummel the bastard for the pain he'd forced Blayze to endure.

But she was right.

He could barely stand. He certainly didn't have the strength to kill a pureblood dragon. Even if the beast was trapped in his spell.

Still, he couldn't resist a parting farewell to the bastard.

Leaning forward, he spoke in a low voice. "It's possible that you will escape death today, unless Synge can figure out what's going on before you escape," he said. "But I promise that I will hunt you down in the future. And I will annihilate you."

Magma released another roar, making Char smile in satisfaction. But before he could continue his smack talk, Blayze was grasping his arm and tugging him away.

"Char, let's go," she commanded.

He allowed himself to be pulled around the curve of the corridor. Okay, it wasn't so much that he *allowed* himself to be led. He was simply incapable of doing anything but stumbling behind Blayze as he struggled to stay upright.

Thankfully, they didn't seem to have far to go as she headed directly toward the ragged hole in the nearby wall.

She stepped over the rubble that filled the corridor. It looked like someone had blasted open the door with a tank. Or a large dragon had gone through it.

"Where's Bolt?" he asked, surprised he couldn't sense the male.

They entered the room where they'd originally arrived in the lair. His eyes widened. It looked decidedly worse for wear. The furniture that had been carefully stacked against the walls was toppled, and a few pieces were completely smashed. Plus the far wall was covered in some nasty goo. The curse?

"He disappeared."

Char came to a startled halt. He couldn't have heard her right. "What did you say?"

She moved to stand only inches from the wall. "He darted in front of me to protect me from the curse," she said. As if that explained everything.

His brows drew together in confusion. "Was he hit with the spell?" he demanded.

She shook her head, walking in a circle with her hand held out in front of her.

"No. Like I said, he disappeared, before the curse reached him."

He felt a stab of concern. Had something happened that had rattled Blayze's senses? She was wandering around in a circle, babbling nonsense, as far as he could tell.

That would explain why she suddenly thought she could get them back home.

"Dragons don't just disappear," he reminded her in a gentle tone.

"Not without help," she said, coming to a sudden halt. "Here."

He moved toward her, intending to pull her out of the room. In a minute, maybe two, his spell holding Magma was going to fail. And when it did, all hell was going to break loose.

They needed to get back to the throne room and hope they could convince Synge to destroy the other dragon.

But even as he reached to grasp her arm, he caught an unexpected scent that lingered in the air. He frowned, sucking in a deep breath.

"It smells like…"

"What?" she demanded as his words trailed away.

It took a second for him to place the evocative odor. "Succubus," he finally announced.

She sent him a startled glance. "Odd. They don't have the power to create portals, do they?"

Like most demons, Char's knowledge of succubi was extremely limited. They tended to remain hidden from the world, appearing to feed off humans before returning to their secluded nests.

"They're a secretive species," he said with a shrug. "I'm not sure what their powers are, beyond being capable of feeding off sexual energy."

Blayze studied him with a searching gaze. "Hmm."

Char blinked, not sure why she was looking at him as if he had a smudge on his face. Then he abruptly realized she thought he'd had a sampling of the succubi's "sexual energy."

He held up a slender hand. "I'm just telling you what I've heard. I don't have any personal experience with a succubus."

Her lips twitched as she returned her attention to a spot directly in front of her. Was she using her magic?

"Perhaps my father commanded her to try and locate me," she said. "He couldn't have known we traveled back in time."

Synge? And a succubus?

This truly was madness.

He lightly touched her shoulder. "What's going on, Blayze?"

"Someone managed to grab Bolt and suck him into…" She gave a small shrug. "Not a portal, precisely. But through a narrow split in time and space." Her features settled into a determined expression. "I can feel the spell that she used. Which means I can grab onto the magic and take us out of here."

There was a tingle in the air, and the speckles of color in Blayze's pale eyes flared with power.

Char hissed in shock. "Wait, Blayze."

The magic continued to pulse in the air as she sent him an impatient frown. "Why?"

He pointed out the obvious. "We don't have any idea where this spell might take us."

She glanced around the dark room, then deliberately allowed her gaze to rest on the sweat that was dripping down his face. A reminder that he was seconds from losing control of an infuriated dragon. "It's better than here."

"There's no guarantee."

She offered a sweet smile, wrapping her arms around his waist.

"Trust me," she whispered.

"Hellfire," he muttered, the room beginning to fade away just as his knees collapsed in exhaustion.

CHAPTER SEVENTEEN

Levet watched as a dark silhouette began to form a few feet from Vex.

Relief crashed through him. Not just that he was not going to be chopped into a pile of gravel by Styx's big sword, but that Blayze was going to be reunited with her family.

From what he'd heard, Blayze had suffered enough.

"Bien!" he said as he rushed forward, his tail twitching with approval. Then the form solidified, and he belatedly realized that this wasn't the pretty female dragon he'd been expecting. Instead it was a large male with long brown hair and dark eyes. Levet skidded to a halt, pointing a claw at the scowling stranger. "Eek. You are not the dragon we wanted."

Tayla gasped, standing next to Levet. But Vex ignored both of them. Her attention was wholly focused on the male standing directly in front of her.

"Bolt?" she whispered.

The dragon's baffled frown was swiftly replaced with something that might have been yearning as he caught sight of the succubus.

"Vex?"

The pretty demon swayed, then she tumbled forward. The dragon cursed before he was moving with blinding speed. He gracefully scooped the unconscious succubus in his arms and cradled her against his chest.

"Stop it, you overgrown lizard." Levet gathered his magic as he moved toward the dragon. He was going to… Well, he didn't know precisely what would happen when he released his power, but it was going to be awesome.

The male that Vex had called Bolt sent him a warning glare. "Stay back."

"What have you done to her?" Levet demanded.

"Me?" Bolt looked horrified by the accusation. "Nothing."

"Then give her to me." Levet held out his arms.

The male tightened his hold on the unconscious succubus. "I will not."

Levet stomped his foot, glaring at the dragon. "Vex is my friend."

A sizzling heat blasted through the room as Bolt cradled Vex even tighter against his chest and shuffled backward. "No." His eyes smoldered, an ebony flame dancing over his long robe. Really, who wore a robe anymore? Levet wrinkled his snout. Only that human dude, the one they called the Pope. "She is mine."

Tayla grabbed the top of his wing, giving him a gentle tug backward.

"Levet. I think they know each other," she said in a

hushed voice. As if she was wary of triggering some violent response from the male.

Levet shook his head. It seemed ridiculous to think that Vex knew some random dragon that she'd plucked from midair. Then again, he'd been in this world long enough to know that fate often interfered at the oddest times.

And Vex had confessed that she had once been in love with a dragon.

Levet narrowed his gaze. "You are the one who broke her heart," he accused.

Bolt glanced down at the female in his arms, his fierce expression melting with an aching regret.

"It was never what I wanted," he rasped. "My father bound my life to another."

Tayla made a sound of impatience. "None of that matters now." She turned to send Levet a frustrated glare. "Vex clearly used her powers to locate her lover. She had no intention of bringing Blayze back to us."

"Blayze?" the male dragon questioned. "Synge's daughter?"

Levet jerked his attention back to Bolt. "You know her?"

The dragon gave a lift of his shoulder. "She was supposed to be my mate."

Levet arched his brows, glancing toward Vex who was snuggled in his arms. "Mate?"

Tayla took a step toward Bolt, her lips parted as if she'd been struck by a sudden thought. "Where did you come from?"

"Synge's lair," he answered without hesitation. "My father and I were there to celebrate the imminent birth of his daughter."

"His daughter?" Tayla widened her eyes. "You mean Blayze?"

"Yes." A strange expression tightened Bolt's

bluntly carved features. "And then a full-grown Blayze appeared."

"Wait." Levet held up his hand, his poor brain spinning as he tried to keep track of what the dragon was telling them. "So you were celebrating your betrothal to the unborn Blayze when the future Blayze showed up?"

Bolt offered a slow, cautious nod, his gaze darting between them and the female who he held with such obvious tenderness.

"Yes, along with her servant Char," he said.

Tayla regarded him with a curious expression. "Did she tell you how she got there? Does she have the ability to travel through time?"

Bolt hesitated, perhaps wondering if they were friend or foe of Blayze. After all, Tayla was an imp and Levet was a gargoyle. They might very well be hunting Blayze for some nefarious purpose.

Then, seeming to sense their genuine concern, he answered. "No. She used her power to follow the curse back to the original caster."

Levet felt a stab of appreciation. He didn't fully understand how Blayze's magic worked, but it was clever of her to trace the curse back in time.

"What happened to her?" Tayla demanded.

"We'd discovered that Magma was plotting to curse her," he said.

The scent of scorched lemons filled the air, making Levet's nose twitch. He didn't even have to glance at Tayla to know she was pissed by the revelation.

"A dragon was responsible for hurting Blayze?" she ground out.

Bolt nodded, his own expression grim. "That was his intent."

Levet wrinkled his snout. Dragons were often bloody in their politics, but most of them were fiercely protective of their offspring. Especially female purebloods. It would be an outrageous breach of etiquette to harm a hatchling. "Why?" he demanded.

Bolt's lips curled with disdain.

"Magma feared his seat on the Council was in jeopardy after he discovered that Synge and my father were negotiating my betrothal to Blayze," Bolt explained.

Ah. Now that sounded more like dragon politics. Strike first and ask questions later.

"He had the curse?" Levet asked.

Bolt shook his head. "No. He bribed Flynn to bring it into the lair."

Levet reached up to scratch his horn. Disappearing dragons. New dragons appearing. Dragons betraying other dragons.

How was he supposed to keep track of what was going on?

"Who is Flynn?" he demanded.

Bolt's disdain deepened. "A vampire in the service of Synge."

Levet parted his lips to demand more information when Tayla suddenly chopped her hand through the air, effectively silencing him.

"We can discuss later who was responsible for the curse," she said, taking command of the situation. "Right now we have to get Blayze back to this time."

Levet gave a helpless lift of his hands. "We cannot do anything until Vex awakens."

Tayla pressed her lips together, waving a hand toward the unconscious succubus. "Can you do something to—"

"No," Bolt interrupted, more flames beginning to swirl around his body. Despite his apparent agitation, however, he was careful to ensure that none of his fire came close to Vex. "She is clearly exhausted," he growled. "I will not have her put in danger."

Tayla jutted her chin to a stubborn angle. "It's not up to you."

Levet studied Vex's pale face. The poor creature was out cold. Clearly she'd used every ounce of her power to bring the dragon through time. It was going to be a while before she revived enough to try again.

Levet turned to grasp Tayla's hand. He understood her urgency.

With each passing second, the threat of a war between the dragons and vampires became more likely.

And the closer he came to being a sacrificial llama. No, wait...lamb. A sacrificial lamb.

"Perhaps it would be best if you travel to Baine and reveal what we have discovered," he urged his friend. Levet might not like Tayla's snarly mate, but he was the most reasonable of all the dragons. Which was not saying much. "If nothing else, you can distract Synge with the information that you discovered the male responsible for having his daughter cursed. By the time Synge hunts down and slaughters Magma, he might be in a more reasonable mood."

Tayla bit her lower lip, offering a slow nod. "True. If he is battling Magma, he can't be at war with the vampires," she agreed.

"And I can live to see another sunrise." Which was really more important than any silly war.

Tayla turned to use her magic, sending Levet a warning glance. "Keep an eye on them."

"Shoo," he said, giving a wave of his hand. She hesitated just a second before forming the portal and disappearing from view. Left alone with the unknown dragon who was eyeing him with a fierce gaze, Levet gave a flap of his wings and puffed out his chest. "Do not try anything funny or I will strike you down with my stupendous magic."

Bolt snapped his brows together, the room heating

with his displeasure. "Has anyone told you that you are an annoying creature?"

Levet sniffed in shocked disbelief at the accusation. "Certainly not. I am beloved by all."

CHAPTER EIGHTEEN

Blayze didn't need any special powers to detect Char's disapproval. It vibrated in the very air. And if she was being honest, she didn't entirely blame him.

Yeah, it was fantastic that they were escaping Magma. And hopefully the spell would take them back through time.

But that didn't keep it from being creepy as hell.

Not only did it feel as if they were treading through thick molasses, but the darkness couldn't be penetrated, not even with their night vision. They would have been completely blind if her natural glow hadn't managed to penetrate the solid sense of nothingness.

And worse, her already depleted magic was beginning to sputter.

She was reaching the limit of her power.

Grimly trying to hide her exhaustion, Blayze felt Char's arms wrap around her waist.

"Stop, Blayze," he commanded, tugging her hard against his body. "I can sense your weariness."

She tilted back her head to meet his worried gaze. "We're close to an opening."

His brooding gaze swept over her face, lingering on her lips.

"Will the spell collapse if we don't get out of here soon?"

She shook her head. The original spell was now completely taken over by her own magic. Otherwise it would have disappeared within a few minutes. "No. Now that I'm manipulating the magic, it will remain stable."

He glanced around, almost as if he was hoping to see through the vast darkness. "What about behind us?"

She blinked, her fatigue making it difficult for her to think clearly. "What do you mean?"

"Can anyone follow us?"

Ah. She understood his confusion. To him it must seem as if they were traveling through a portal. Instead, she was ripping through the threads of time, using magic from the succubus as her compass.

Which meant there was no way for anyone to trace their passage.

"No, there's no way anyone can reach us," she assured him.

"Good. Then you're going to rest."

She wrinkled her nose, trying to pretend as if she wasn't about to collapse. "Are you giving me orders?"

"Yes."

Without warning, Char closed his eyes. Blayze frowned as she felt the warmth of his power brushing over her. At first she assumed he was trying to share his power with her, then the darkness began to pulse as a dome of light spread around them.

Her breath caught as there was a sudden shimmer in

the air, and in the blink of an eye, the area was transformed from the bleak shadows to a gorgeous bedchamber.

There was a smooth marble floor and white fluted pillars that held up a mosaic-tiled ceiling. The walls were decorated with delicate tapestries. And in the very center of the space was a large four-poster bed draped in golden silk. It looked like something out of a fairy tale.

Or more likely, her deepest fantasies.

Dragons were capable of creating illusions that seemed real. And the most powerful dragons could reach into the mind of another to create what they most desired. But she'd never heard of a half-breed possessing the talent.

Clearly, Char was even more powerful than she'd suspected.

Busy appreciating their lovely surroundings, Blayze was caught off guard when Char swept her off her feet. He stared down at her startled expression as he crossed the floor. Then, with a sudden smile he tossed her into the center of the vast bed.

She landed on the soft mattress, her arms and legs splayed like a sacrificial virgin.

Which she technically was.

Oh, not the sacrificial part. Just the virgin part.

Suddenly Blayze forgot all about her weariness. Instead, a heart-stopping pleasure sizzled through her body as she allowed her gaze to skim over the male standing next to the bed.

He was just so gorgeous. His short hair that gleamed like polished silver. His gray eyes that had softened to mist. The elegant features that held a hint of his fey blood.

She knew she could search for the rest of eternity and never find another male who could ignite her blood to such a fever pitch.

Almost on cue, her dragon stirred and stretched, purring in anticipation. "What if I'm not in the mood to rest?"

His eyes darkened, his nose flaring as he caught the unmistakable scent of her arousal. Still, he visibly struggled to keep his own dragon leashed.

"Please, Blayze, you're tired." His voice was thick with strain. "I need you to take care of yourself."

She moved until she was perched on her knees in the center of the bed. Then, holding his gaze, she reached down to grasp her beaded gown, sliding it over her head.

"You're killing me," Char rasped, silver flames dancing around him as she tossed the gown aside to reveal her naked body.

She tilted her head to the side, trying to look provocative. "A succubus created the original spell we're following," she pointed out. "Which means there's only one way to truly recharge my magic."

It wasn't actually true. Oh, there might be a way to tap into sexual energy if it lingered in the spell. But she knew Char intended to be annoyingly noble. He was convinced that he was somehow unworthy to be her mate because of his mixed bloodline.

Which meant she had to do whatever necessary to prove that none of that stuff mattered to her.

Or to her dragon.

His gaze roamed down her naked body, his eyes glittering like shards of silver.

"Your father—"

She leaned forward, placing her hand across his mouth. "No."

Char reached up to wrap his fingers around her wrist, gently tugging her hand away. "If we manage to return home, we both know that your father will expect you to accept his choice of a mate."

Blayze shook her head. She didn't care if she had to go back into hiding. She was never, ever going to hand control of her life over to another.

Especially not Synge.

"We *will* return," she insisted. "And when we do, I will inform my father that I've already chosen my mate."

Char's breath hissed through his teeth, his beast visible in his eyes. "Mate?"

A slow smile curved her lips. "Mate."

"You're certain."

"More certain than I have ever been in my life," she assured him in a husky voice. "I belong with you."

Kicking off his heavy shoes, Char ripped off his shirt and dropped his slacks to reveal the breathtaking glory of his male form.

"Synge won't be happy," he growled, moving to join her on the mattress.

Blayze's brain threatened to shut down as she reached out to touch the smooth, chiseled muscles of his chest. Not that she cared. Surely a female wasn't supposed to think when she was in the presence of a naked male?

Her dragon roared and her palm sizzled from the heat of his flames.

"Synge's ability to make decisions for my future was ended when he condemned me to death," she reminded him.

He shivered as her fingers stroked over the broad width of his chest.

"What about your mother?" he demanded.

"I love her, of course." She shrugged. "And I will be eternally grateful for the sacrifices she made for me. But it's time for her to live her own life." Her hand skimmed downward, exploring the rigid hardness of his abs. *Very nice.* Then she explored lower, wrapping her fingers around his thick erection. *Even nicer.* "And allow me to live my life."

A groan was wrenched from Char's lips as she pressed her hand down the long length of his cock. She smiled. Her dragon liked that. She pulled her fingers back to the tip, using her thumb to tease at the sensitive head before she pushed back down again.

His flames scorched over her as he lowered her back onto the golden silk blanket and covered her with his body.

"Does living your life include me?" he asked in husky tones.

"If you want me." She lifted her hands to wrap them around his neck, her flames igniting to dance like iridescent jewels between them.

It was the first time she'd ever had her fire kindled by desire.

It was intoxicating.

"Want?" Swooping his head downward, Char nibbled at the corner of her mouth. "That doesn't begin to describe my need for you."

A violent shudder shook her body, the beast inside her pressing against her skin in an effort to get closer to Char.

Dear goddess, she wanted to consume him.

From the top of his silvery head to the tip of his toes. And every single inch in between.

"Then what would describe your need?" she asked, her fingers tracing the wide width of his shoulders.

"I ache to taste your lips," Char growled low in his throat, his hands moving restlessly over her bare skin before he covered her mouth in a deep kiss. A ruthless hunger scorched through Blayze, making her body arch at the sheer intensity. Char moaned his approval, his mouth moving to scatter tiny kisses over her flushed face. "I hunger to feel your body pressed against mine."

Mmm.

The hot male scent of his dragon spiced the air.

"It's a start," she assured him.

He offered a throaty laugh. "Ah, a demanding female," he rasped, allowing one of his hands to slide between her thighs and stroke through her damp heat.

Her nails scored down Char's back, pleasure searing through her.

"I have a lot of time to make up for," she reminded him.

He crushed her lips in another demanding kiss. "We have all eternity." He lifted his head, staring down at her as he pressed his finger into her tight flesh. "We do have all eternity, don't we? Once I claim you there's no way I'm going to let you go."

Blayze instinctively dug her heels into the mattress beneath her as she tilted her hips upward.

"Yes," she breathed, her dragon twisting restlessly beneath her flesh. His finger was creating the most delicious friction as he dipped it in and out of her. "Char."

He nibbled kisses over her cheek, then down the length of her jaw. "Tell me you're certain, Blayze." He stroked the tip of his tongue over the pulse racing at the base of her throat. "I need to hear the words."

"Without a doubt," she assured him, not hesitating for even a beat. Her hands moved down the curve of his spine, stroking his flames higher and higher. "Now tell me more about how much you want me."

"I lust for you." His mouth trailed down her collarbone. "For the softness of your body." He lapped at the aching tip of her breast. "The heat of your dragon."

A moan fell from her parted lips. This game was swiftly spiraling out of control. In the most delicious way.

"Like this?" she asked softly, releasing a breath of

her dragon-fire.

His entire body quivered. Not from pain. His expression was one of pure bliss.

"Exactly like that," he rasped, using the edge of his teeth to torment her sensitive nipple.

Fisting her fingers in his thick hair, she instinctively wrapped her legs around his hips.

"This is…" Her words lodged in her throat.

Pulling back, he regarded her with a searching gaze. "What?"

She instinctively rubbed herself against the hot length of his erection.

"So much more than I dreamed it would be."

His eyes darkened to smoke, the power of his dragon beating against her. "Yes." Bearing his weight on his elbows, Char angled his hips until the tip of his cock pressed against her entrance. "More than I ever dreamed possible."

Her dragon huffed with impatience. She might not have experience, but her body understood what it needed. And that it needed it now.

"So why are you waiting?" she demanded, digging her nails into his back as he studied her with an oddly intense expression.

"There's something I want to give you first."

She blinked in confusion. Most dragons were obsessed with adding to their hoards, but she'd already told Char that she had no interest in possessions.

All she'd ever wanted was to be rid of the curse.

And to find her mate.

"I really don't want—"

Her words ended on a gasp as she felt a tingle of power wrap around her, and a delicate weight lying against her upper chest. Glancing down, she caught sight of the golden necklace that gleamed in the glow of her skin.

Despite her seclusion from the world, she knew exactly what it was.

A dragon marque.

A symbol of ownership. Or in this case, a symbol of Char's intention to claim her as a mate.

She breathed out a soft sigh as her fingers stroked over the precious metal. She could feel the power of his dragon in the marque, as well as the effervescent fey magic.

"Char." She moved her hand to lightly stroke her fingers over his lips. "Right now, I truly wish you could freeze time for all eternity. There has never been a more perfect moment."

A wicked smile touched his lips. "I promise it's going to get a lot more perfect."

She wasn't entirely sure what he meant. Not until Char pushed his hips forward, sliding into her with a slow, relentless thrust.

Releasing a breath of pleasure, Blayze clutched at Char's shoulders, her nails digging into his skin. There wasn't pain. Her body was ready and willing to accommodate his entry. But there was a splendid sense of fullness, and a shocking intimacy.

She'd craved this male since she'd opened her eyes to find him hovering above her.

Now that she finally had him plunging deep inside her, she realized that it was a craving that would never, ever end.

Perhaps sensing the profound emotions that were thundering through her, Char buried his face in the curve of her neck.

"Blayze," he whispered. "Hold on tight."

"I'm never letting go," she promised. "Just don't stop."

He released a choked laugh. "Trust me, there's no way in hell I'm stopping," he told her, pulling out of her body before thrusting back in with a growing urgency. "You've promised to be mine."

"And you are mine," she groaned as he began moving with a rhythm that stole her breath.

Yes. Oh, yes. This was what her body had ached to feel during the centuries she'd been locked away. This was what she needed.

Allowing her eyes to shut, Blayze growled in pleasure as his teeth sank into her neck. He rocked into her faster and faster, his hands grasping her hips to hold her in place as his pounding thrusts threatened to send her off the mattress.

"Harder," she muttered against his lips, her body clenched so tightly she felt as if she might shatter.

"You're glowing." Kissing a path down her throat, he skimmed his lips between the swell of her breasts as he allowed his dragon-fire to sear over her sensitive skin.

Blayze's rasping breath was the only sound to disturb the silent air, her world narrowing to the point where Char's body surged in and out of her.

She was swiftly careening toward a distant goal, her back arched and her fingers digging into Char's back.

And then…it happened.

With one last surge he tumbled her over the edge, sending her spinning with a tidal wave of dizzying bliss.

He claimed her lips in a searing kiss, continuing to pump into her shuddering body until he went rigid with his own release. Then, as he shouted out at the force of his climax, their flames combusted around them.

Her eyes slowly opened, a sated pleasure settling over her with a delicious sense of peace.

"Char."

***

Levet sighed, preparing to make his way to the

portal that Tayla had created for him just outside Synge's lair.

He should be delighted.

What had the great bard said? "All's well that ends well."

And everything had certainly ended well.

Blayze and Char had safely returned from their journey back in time. And not only had Blayze managed to get rid of her curse, but she'd mated with Char. Something that might have pissed off Synge if the older dragon wasn't busy destroying Magma and his clan.

Bolt had been reunited with his grieving father, who'd been so relieved to have him back that he hadn't even protested when Bolt insisted that Vex was going to be his mate.

And Baine had just returned from The Viper Pit to command that Tayla travel with him to their private lair, so they could enjoy some "alone time."

So why was he feeling azure? No, wait…blue. *Oui.* Why was he feeling blue?

His gaze skimmed over the crowd that filled Synge's throne room, lingering on the couples who were clinging to each other like they might suddenly be pulled apart.

Char and Blayze, both glowing in the lovely light from Blayze's skin. Vex and Bolt, who could barely look at anyone but each other. And Tayla and Baine, who were playing kissy-face in a dark corner.

Then he wrinkled his snout. It was well known that he was a romantic at heart. And he was truly delighted with all the happy endings. But he could not deny a hint of envy.

Had he not been the one to create the happily-ever-afters for everyone?

So where was his?

Giving a click of his tongue at his unusual bout of

self-pity, Levet spread his wings and turned to leave the lair, then stepped to enter the portal. Tayla had promised him that it would take him to where his heart most desired to go.

He was very much hoping that meant a one-way trip to his lovely fire imp who he'd abandoned when Tayla had first called for him.

Darkness surrounded him, and Levet felt himself being whisked away. There was a strange sense of disorientation as he floated in space, then, with a violent bump, he landed on a hard floor.

Shoving himself to his feet, he scowled as he rubbed his scuffed *derrière*. The portal had clearly been defective. Otherwise he would have landed with his usual graceful style.

As if to prove his point, he glanced around the dark room, quickly realizing this was not a cozy bedchamber beneath a volcano.

Non. This was…the cellars beneath The Viper Pit.

His tail suddenly twitched, his annoyance evaporating as he scurried toward wooden shelves that were lined with bottles.

Viper's private stash!

Wine. Champagne. Bourbon. Tequila. Even an entire barrel of nectar.

Ah. This was precisely what a weary gargoyle needed after stopping a war, and ensuring a happy ending for all.

Grabbing a ladle that was set on one of the shelves, Levet scurried toward the barrel and pried off the top. Then, dipping the ladle in the golden liquid, he lifted it to his lips to take a deep swallow.

Instantly his muscles loosened and his wings fluttered in pleasure. *Sweet, sweet nectar.*

The drink of the gods. And miniature gargoyles.

He'd almost managed to polish off the entire ladle

and was enjoying a dizzying buzz of euphoria when a cold chill snaked its way through the cellar.

"Who's down here?" Viper's familiar voice echoed through the air.

Levet slapped his hand over his mouth as he stifled a giggle.

Not that it helped. Viper was a vampire who had an uncanny ability to sense when someone was tapping into his cache of expensive spirits.

"Do I smell granite?" Viper rasped, the crunch of his footsteps coming closer and closer. "Levet, I'm going to kill you."

Levet released a hiccup and dipped the ladle back into the nectar. If he was going to die, he was going to do it with a smile on his face.

Pretend you're safe

by Alexandra Ivy

PROLOGUE

Frank Johnson had endured his fair share of floods. He'd been born and raised on the small farm that butted against the bank of the Mississippi River. Which meant he'd spent the past sixty years watching the muddy waters rise and fall. Sometimes sweeping away crops, cattle, and during one memorable year, the barn that had been built by his great-grandfather.

The levee that'd been built by the Corps of Engineers over a decade ago had provided a measure of security. Not that he'd been happy when they'd come in and scooped up his fertile land to create the barrier. Frank was a typical Midwestern farmer who didn't need the government poking their noses, or bulldozers, into his business. But eventually he'd had to admit it was nice not to have the waters lapping at the back door every time it rained.

But this was no typical rain.

On the first of February the heavens had opened up and six weeks later, the torrential rains continued to pound the small community. The river had become an angry, churning, destructive force as it swept toward the south. Frank watched in resignation as the water had inched closer and closer to the top of the levee. He knew it was only a matter of time before it spilled over the ridge and into his back field.

But when he woke that morning, it wasn't to find the levee had been topped. Nope. It had been busted wide open. As if someone had set off an explosion during the night.

With the resignation of a man who'd lived his entire life dependent on the fickleness of nature, he'd pulled on his coveralls and boots before firing up his old tractor and heading down to see the damage.

Dawn had arrived, but the thick clouds and persistent drizzle shrouded the farm in a strange gloom. Frank pulled the collar of his coveralls up to protect his neck from the chilled breeze, starting to feel like Noah. Had he missed the memo from God that he was supposed to build an ark?

The inane thought had barely formed in his mind when he allowed the tractor to roll to a halt. As expected, his fields had become pools of brown, brackish water. In some places the nasty stuff was waist deep. There were also the usual leaves, branches, and pieces of flotsam that'd been caught in the swirling eddies.

What he hadn't expected was the long, dark object that he spotted floating in the middle of his pasture.

His first thought had been that it was a log. Maybe a piece of lumber torn from a building. But a piece of wood wouldn't make his stomach cramp with a sense of dread, would it?

Climbing off his tractor, he'd reached into his pocket for his cell phone. His unconscious mind had already warned him that whatever the floodwaters had washed onto his land was going to be bad.

And it was.

Really, really bad.

CHAPTER ONE

First came the floods. And then the bodies...

Jaci Patterson was running late.

It all started when she woke at her usual time of four a.m. Yes, she really and truly woke at that indecent hour, five days a week. On the weekends, she allowed herself to sleep in until six. But this morning, when she crawled out of bed, she discovered the electricity was out.

Again.

The lack of power had nothing to do with the sketchy electrical lines that ran to her remote farmhouse in the northeast corner of Missouri. At least not this time. Instead, it could be blamed on the rains that continued to hammer the entire Midwest day after day.

When the lights grudgingly flickered on an hour later, she had to rush through her routine, grateful that she'd baked two dozen peach tarts and several loaves of bread the night before.

As it was she'd barely managed to finish her blueberry muffins and scones before she had to load them into the back of her Jeep. Then, locking her two black labs, Riff and Raff, in the barn so they didn't destroy her house while she was gone, she headed

173

toward Heron, the small town just ten miles away.

Predictably, she was barreling down the muddy lane that led to the small farm that'd once belonged to her grandparents, when she discovered the road was blocked before she could reach the intersection. *Crap.* Obviously the levee had broken during the night, releasing the swollen fury of the Mississippi River.

It was no wonder her electricity had gone out.

Grimacing at the knowledge that her bottom fields, along with most of her neighbors', were probably flooded, she put the Jeep in reverse. Then, careful to stay in the center of the muddy road, she reversed her way back to the lane. Once she managed to get turned around, she headed in the opposite direction.

The detour took an extra fifteen minutes, but at least she didn't have to worry about traffic. With fewer than three hundred people, Heron wasn't exactly a hub of activity. In fact, she ran into exactly zero cars as she swung along Main Street.

She splashed through the center of town that was lined with a small post office, the county courthouse that was built in the eighteen hundreds with a newer jail that had been added onto the back, a bank, and a beauty parlor. On the opposite side was the Baptist church and next to it a two-story brick building that the local celebrity, Nelson Bradley, had converted into a gallery for his photographs. Further down the block was a newly constructed tin shed that housed the fire truck and the water department. On the corner was a small diner that had originally been christened the Cozy Kitchen, but had slowly become known as the Bird's Nest by the locals after it'd been taken over by Nancy Bird, or Birdie, as she was affectionately nicknamed.

Pulling into the narrow alley behind the diner, Jaci hopped out of her vehicle to grab the top container of muffins that were still warm from the oven. Instantly, she regretted not pulling on her jacket as the drizzling rain molded her short honey brown hair to her scalp and dampened her Mizzou sweatshirt and faded jeans to her generously curved body.

With a shiver she hurried through the back door, careful to wipe the mud from her rubber boots before entering the kitchen.

Heat smacked her in the face, the contrast from the chilled wind outside making the cramped space feel smothering.

Grimacing, she walked to set the muffins on a narrow stainless steel table that was next to the griddle filled with scrambled eggs, hash browns, sausage and sizzling bacon.

The large woman with graying hair and a plump face efficiently flipped a row of pancakes before gesturing toward the woman who was standing at the sink washing dishes. Once the helper had hurried to her side, she handed off her spatula and made her way toward Jaci.

Nancy Bird, better known as Birdie, was fifteen years older than Jaci. When she was just seventeen she'd married her high school sweetheart and dropped out of school. The sweetheart turned out to be a horse patootie who'd fled town, leaving Birdie with four young girls to raise on her own.

With a determination that Jaci deeply admired, Birdie had bought the old diner and over the past ten years turned it into the best place to eat in the entire county.

At this early hour her clients usually consisted of farmers, hunters and school bus drivers who were up before dawn.

"Morning, Birdie." Jaci stepped aside as the older woman efficiently began to place the muffins on a large glass tray that would be set on the counter next to the cash register. Many of the diners liked to have a cup of coffee and muffin once they were done with breakfast.

"Thank God you're here."

"I'm sorry I'm late. The electricity didn't come on until almost five."

Finishing, Birdie grabbed the tray and bustled across the kitchen to hand it to her assistant.

"Take this to the counter," Birdie commanded before turning back to Jaci with a roll of her eyes. "The natives have been threatening to revolt without their favorite muffins."

Jaci smiled, pleased by Birdie's words. She'd learned to bake at her grandmother's side, but it wasn't until she'd inherited her grandparents' farm that she'd considered using her skills to help her make ends meet.

Leaning to the side she glanced through the large open space where the food was passed through to the waitresses.

The place hadn't changed in the past ten years. The walls were covered with faded paneling that was decorated with old license plates and a mounted fish caught from the nearby river. The floor was linoleum with a drop ceiling that was lit with fluorescent lights.

There was a half dozen tables arranged around the square room with one long table at the back where a group of farmers showed up daily to drink coffee and share the local gossip.

At the moment, every seat was filled with patrons wearing buff coveralls, camo jackets, and Cardinal baseball hats.

Jaci released a slow whistle. "Damn, woman. That's quite a crowd," she said, a rueful smile touching her lips. The rains meant that no one was able to get into the fields. "At least someone can benefit from this latest downpour."

"Benefit?" Birdie sucked in a sharp breath, her

hands landing on her generous hips. "I hope you're not suggesting that I'm the sort of person who enjoys benefitting from a tragedy, Jaci Patterson," she chastised. "People want to get together to discuss what's happened and I have the local spot for them to gather."

Jaci blinked, caught off guard by her friend's sharp reprimand. Then, absorbing the older woman's words, she stiffened in concern.

"Tragedy?" she breathed.

Birdie's features softened. "You haven't heard?"

Jaci felt a tremor of unease. She'd already lost her father to a drunk driver before she was even born, and then her grandmother when she was seventeen. Her grandfather had passed just two years ago. She was still raw from their deaths.

"No, I haven't heard anything. Like I said, the electricity went out last night and as soon as it come back on I started baking. Has someone died?"

"I'm afraid so."

"Who?"

"No one knows for sure yet," Birdie told her.

Jaci blinked in confusion. "How could they not know?"

"The levee broke in the middle of the night."

"Yeah, I figured that out when I discovered that the road was closed…oh hell." She tensed as her unease became sharp-edged fear. The levee had broken before and flooded fields, but the neighbor to her south had recently built a new house much closer to the river. "It didn't reach Frank's home, did it?"

Birdie shook her head. "Just the back pasture."

"Then what body are you talking about?"

"When Frank went to check on the breach, he saw something floating in the middle of his field."

Jaci cringed. Poor Frank. He must have been shocked out of his mind.

"Oh my God. It was a dead person?"

"Yep. A woman."

"He didn't recognize her?"

Birdie leaned forward and lowered her voice, as if anyone could hear over the noise from the customers, not to mention the usual kitchen clatter.

"He said it was impossible to know if she was familiar or not."

"I don't suppose he wanted to look too close," Jaci said. If she'd spotted a body in her flooded field she would have jumped into her Jeep and driven away like a maniac.

"It wasn't that. He claimed the woman was too..." Birdie hesitated, as if she was searching for a more delicate way to express what Frank had said. "Decomposed to make out her features."

"Decomposed?" A strange chill inched down Jaci's spine.

"That's what he's saying."

Jaci absently glanced through the opening into the outer room where she could see Frank surrounded by a group of avid listeners.

When Birdie had said a body, she'd assumed it had been someone who'd been caught in the flood. Maybe she'd fallen in when she was walking along the bank. Or her car might had been swept away when she tried to cross a road with high water.

But she wouldn't be decomposed, would she?

"I've heard that water does strange things to a body," Jaci at last said.

Birdie tugged Jaci toward the back door as her assistant moved to open the fridge. Clearly there was more to the story.

"The body wasn't all that Frank discovered."

Jaci stilled. "There was more?"

"Yep." Birdie whispered, as if it was a big secret.

Which was ridiculous. There were no such things as secrets in a town the size of Heron. "Frank called the sheriff and while he was waiting for Mike to arrive he swears he caught sight of a human skull stuck in the mud at the edge of the road." Birdie gave a horrified shudder. "Can you imagine? Two dead people virtually in his backyard? Gives me the creeps just thinking about it."

Jaci's mouth went dry. "Did Frank say anything else?"

Birdie shrugged. "Just that the sheriff told him to leave and not to talk about what he found." Birdie snorted. "Like anyone wouldn't feel the need to share the fact they found a dead body and a skull in their field."

A familiar dread curdled in the pit of her stomach.

She was being an idiot. Of course she was. This had nothing to do with her past. Or the mysterious stalker who had made her life hell.

Still…

She couldn't shake the sudden premonition that slithered down her spine.

"Is Mike still out at Frank's?" she abruptly demanded, referring to the sheriff, Mike O'Brien.

"Yeah." Birdie sent her a curious glance. "I think he was waiting for the Corps of Engineers to get out there so they could discuss how long it would take for the field to drain." She wrinkled her nose. "I suppose they need to make sure there aren't any other bodies."

More bodies.

A fierce urgency pounded through her. She might be overreacting, but she wasn't going to be satisfied until she spoke to Mike.

"I need to go."

"You haven't had your coffee," Birdie protested.

"Not this morning, thanks, Birdie."

"Okay." The older woman stepped back. "I'll get

your money and-"

"I'll stop by later to get it." Jaci turned to pull open the back door.

Instantly a chilled blast of air swept around them.

"What's your rush?" Birdie demanded.

"I have some questions that need answers," she said.

"With who?" Birdie demanded, making a sound of impatience as Jaci darted into the alley and jogged toward her waiting Jeep. "Jaci?"

Not bothering to answer, Jaci jumped into the vehicle and put it in gear. Water trickled down her neck from her wet hair, but when she'd gone into the diner she'd left the engine running with the heater blasting at full steam.

Which meant she was a damp mess, but she wasn't completely miserable.

Angling the vent in a futile effort to dry her soggy sweatshirt, Jaci stomped on the accelerator and headed back toward her house. This time, however, she swerved around the barrier that blocked the road, squishing her way through the muddy path that led along the edge of Frank's property.

It was less than ten miles, but by the time she was pulling her vehicle to a halt, her stomach had managed to clench into a tight ball of nerves.

It didn't matter how many times she told herself that this had nothing to do with the past, she couldn't dismiss her rising tide of fear.

Ignoring the avid crowd of onlookers who were gathered at the edge of the field, Jaci skirted around the wooden barrier, her gaze skimming over the sluggish brown water that had surged through the broken levee. Branches and debris swirled through the field. But no body.

Thank God.

"Jaci," a male voice intruded into her distracted thoughts as a skinny man dressed in a dark uniform stepped in front of her.

She forced a smile to her lips. "Morning, Sid."

The young deputy nodded his head toward the flooded field, trying to look suitably somber.

"I guess you heard the news?"

"Yep." Jaci's gaze moved over the deputy's shoulder, landing on the man who was pacing along the edge of the road with a cell phone pressed to his ear.

Sheriff Mike O'Brien.

Only a year older than Jaci's twenty-seven, he was wearing a crisp black uniform with a star on his sleeve that indicated his elected status. Beneath his shirt he was wearing body armor that emphasized his broad, muscular frame. He had light brown hair that he kept cut military-short beneath his black ball cap, and a square face with blunt features and eyes that were an astonishing shade of green. As bright as fresh mint.

He was the sort of solid, dependable man that Jaci had always told herself she should want. Which explained why she'd dated him for several months after returning to Heron.

Unfortunately, they just hadn't...clicked. At least not for her. Mike continued to ask her out. She didn't know if he was truly smitten with her, or if she was a convenient date.

After all, Heron wasn't overrun with eligible women.

"I think half the town is here to gawk." Sid once again interrupted her thoughts, his chest puffed out. It was a rare treat to have so much excitement. Jaci, however, was intent on reaching Mike. She stepped around the barrier, neatly avoiding Sid's attempt to grab her arm. "Wait," he commanded.

She marched forward, the mud threatening to suck

off her rubber boots.

"I need to speak with Mike," she said, battling her way toward her friend.

Sid made an effort to block her path. "The sheriff closed off this area. He said he didn't want no one here disturbing things until he finished up."

She darted around him. She was nothing if not determined. "I'll just be a minute."

"But-"

"Don't worry, Sid," she called over her shoulder. "I won't disturb anything."

Realizing he was going to have to physically wrestle her to the ground if he hoped to stop her, Sid returned to his post beside the barrier.

"He's going to put my balls in a vise," he groused.

KILL WITHOUT SHAME
(ARES SECURITY)

BY ALEXANDRA IVY

CHAPTER ONE

The Saloon was the sort of bar that catered to the locals in the quiet Houston neighborhood.

It was small, with lots of wood and polished brass. Overhead there was an open beam ceiling, with muted lights that provided a cozy atmosphere, and on the weekends they invited a jazz band to play quietly on the narrow stage.

Lucas spent most Friday evenings at the table tucked in a back corner. It was unofficially reserved for the five men who ran ARES Security.

The men liked the peaceful ambiance, the communal agreement that everyone should mind their own business, and the fact that the table was situated so no one could sneak up from behind.

Trained soldiers didn't want surprises.

At the moment, the bar was nearly empty. Not only was it a gray, wet Wednesday evening, but it was the first week of December. That meant Christmas madness was in full swing.

Perfectly normal people were now in crazy-mode as they scurried from store to store, battling one another for the latest, have-to-have gift. It was like Thunderdome without Tina Turner.

Currently Lucas and Teagan shared the bar with a

young couple seated near the bay window at the front of the bar. Those two were oblivious to everything but each other. And closer to the empty stage was a table of college girls. Already at the giggly stage of drunk, they were all blatantly checking him out. At least when they weren't gawking at Teagan.

No biggie.

Both men were accustomed to female attention.

Teagan was a large, heavily muscled man with dark caramel skin, and golden eyes that he'd inherited from his Polynesian mother. He kept his hair shaved close to his skull, and as usual was dressed in a pair of camo pants and shit-kickers. He had an aggressive vibe that was only emphasized by the tight T-shirt that left his arms bare to reveal the numerous tattoos.

Lucas St. Clair, on the other hand, was wearing a thousand-dollar suit that was tailored to perfectly fit his lean body. His glossy black hair was smoothed away from his chiseled face that he'd been told could easily grace the covers of fashion magazines. As if he gave a shit.

His eyes were so dark they looked black. It wasn't until he was in the sunlight that it became obvious they were a deep, indigo blue.

Most assumed he was the less dangerous of the two men.

They'd be wrong.

But while the girls became increasingly more obvious in their attempts to attract their attention, neither man glanced in their direction.

Teagan because he already had a flock of women who included supermodels and two famous actresses.

And Lucas because... He grimaced.

To be honest, he wasn't sure why. He only knew that his interest in women hadn't been the same since he'd crawled out of that hellhole in Afghanistan. Not unless he counted the hours he spent brooding on one woman in particular.

The one who got away.

Lucas gave a sharp shake of his head, reaching for his shot of tequila. It slid down his throat like liquid fire, burning away the past.

Nothing like a twelve-year-old vintage to ease the pain.

Lucas glanced toward his companion's empty glass.

"Another round?" he asked.

"Sure." Teagan waited for Lucas to nod toward the bartender, who was washing glasses, at the same time keeping a sharp eye on his few customers. "I assume you're picking up the tab?"

Lucas cocked a brow. "Why do I always have to pick up the tab?"

"You're the one with the trust fund, amigo, not me," Teagan said with a shrug. "The only thing my father ever gave me was a concussion and an intimate knowledge of the Texas penal system."

Lucas snorted. It was common knowledge that Lucas would beg in the streets before he would touch a penny of the St. Clair fortune. Just as they all knew that Teagan had risen above his abusive background, and temporary housing in the penitentiary, to become a successful businessman. The younger man not only joined ARES, but he owned a mechanic shop that catered to a high-end clientele who had more money than sense when it came to their precious sports cars.

"I might break out the violins if I didn't know you're making a fortune," Lucas told his friend as the bartender arrived to replace their drinks with a silent efficiency.

"Hardly a fortune." Teagan downed a shot of tequila before he reached for his beer, heaving a faux sigh. "I have overhead out the ass, not to mention paying my cousins twice what they're worth. A word of warning, amigo. Never go into business with your family."

"Too late," Lucas murmured.

As far as he was concerned, the men who crawled out of that Taliban cave with him were his brothers. And the only family that mattered.

"True that." Teagan gave a slow nod, holding up his frosty glass. "To ARES."

Lucas clinked his glass against Teagan's in appreciation of the bond they'd formed.

"To ARES."

Drinking the tequila in one swallow, Lucas set aside his empty glass. There was a brief silence before Teagan at last spoke the words that'd no doubt been on the tip of his tongue since they walked through the door of the bar.

"Are you ever going to get to the point of why you asked to meet me here?" his friend bluntly demanded.

Lucas leaned back in his chair, arching his brows.

"Couldn't it just be because I enjoy your sparkling personality?"

Teagan snorted. "If I'd known this was a date I would have worn my lucky shirt."

"You need a shirt to get lucky?"

"Not usually." Teagan flashed his friend a mocking smile. "But I've heard you like to play hard to get."

Lucas grimaced at the direct hit. Yeah. Hard to get was one way to put it.

"I want to discuss Hauk," he admitted, not at all eager to think about his lack of a sex life.

ABOUT THE AUTHOR

Alexandra Ivy is a *New York Times* and *USA Today* bestselling author of the Guardians of Eternity, as well as the Sentinels, Dragons of Eternity and ARES series. After majoring in theatre she decided she prefers to bring her characters to life on paper rather than stage. She lives in Missouri with her family. Visit her website at www.alexandraivy.com.

Made in the USA
San Bernardino, CA
24 April 2017